# BEOWULF
## BEASTSLAYER

*Beowulf Beastslayer* is unlike other books. In fact, it is a gateway to the mythic world of the Scandinavian sagas, an age of heroes and monsters. Once inside its pages, you will find yourself transported to King Hrothgar's golden hall of Heorot to embark upon a thrilling adventure of your own.

In addition to the book itself, you will need two six-sided dice (or a standard pack of playing cards), a pencil and an eraser. Using these tools, and a simple set of game rules contained within the book, you will take on the role of the first superhero of the English literary tradition – the beastslayer Beowulf – in an inventive reimagining of the Anglo-Saxon epic.

YOU decide which route to take, which perils to risk, and which of the strange creatures you will meet along the way to engage in combat. But whether you survive your quest and rise to the level of lauded hero, and maybe even king, or succumb to the likes of the monster Grendel and his sea-hag mother, will be down to the choices YOU make.

*Beowulf Beastslayer!* A tale of heroes... A tale of monsters... A legend reborn!

Proudly Published by Snowbooks in 2019

Snowbooks Ltd.
email: info@snowbooks.com
www.snowbooks.com

British Library Cataloguing in Publication Data
A catalogue record for this book is available from the British
Library.

Hardcover 9781911390732
Paperback 9781911390664
Ebook 9781911390671

With thanks to the Play-Testers of Heorot:
Kevin Abbotts, James A Hirons, Andrew Alvis, Simon Day,
Kola "I hate luminous moss" Krauze,
Allan Matthews, Lars Quante, René Batsford,
Mark "Daelhoof" Johnson, Furrida, Fabrice Gatille,
Eddie Boshell, Edward J. Kulzer, Prof. Dr. Oliver M. Traxel,
Jason Vince (Dreamwalker Spirit),
林立人 Lin Liren, Simon Scott, Luca Meregalli,
Gonçalo Rodrigues, David Poppel, and Ron Bishop.

With special thanks to Paul Simpson

# BEOWULF
## BEASTSLAYER

## by Jonathan Green

## Illustrated by Russ Nicholson

SNOWBOOKS

## Also by Jonathan Green

### ACE Gamebooks
*Alice's Nightmare in Wonderland*
*The Wicked Wizard of Oz*
*NEVERLAND – Here Be Monsters!*
*'TWAS – The Krampus Night Before Christmas*

### Snowbooks Fantasy Histories
*You Are The Hero – A History of Fighting Fantasy Gamebooks*
*You Are The Hero Part 2*

### Snowbooks Anthologies
*Sharkpunk* (edited by Jonathan Green)
*Game Over* (edited by Jonathan Green)
*Shakespeare Vs Cthulhu* (edited by Jonathan Green)

### Fighting Fantasy Gamebooks
*Spellbreaker*
*Knights of Doom*
*Curse of the Mummy*
*Bloodbones*
*Howl of the Werewolf*
*Stormslayer*
*Night of the Necromancer*

**Sonic the Hedgehog Adventure Gamebooks**
*Theme Park Panic* (with Marc Gascoigne)
*Stormin' Sonic* (with Marc Gascoigne)

**Doctor Who Adventure Gamebooks**
*Decide Your Destiny: The Horror of Howling Hill*
*Choose The Future: Night of the Kraken*

**Star Wars: The Clone Wars – Decide Your Destiny**
*Crisis on Coruscant*

**Gamebook Adventures**
*Temple of the Spider God*

**Warlock's Bounty**
*Revenge of the Sorcerer*

**Path to Victory**
*Herald of Oblivion*
*Shadows Over Sylvania*

# In Memoriam

I first encountered the monster Grendel in Carey Miller's *A Dictionary of Monsters and Mysterious Beasts* (first published in 1974), alongside other such legendary creatures as the Abominable Snowman, the Cockatrice, and the Lambton Worm. I would spend hours copying out the encyclopaedic entries from that book onto sheets of lined paper, using my Berol felt-tip pens.

The way Grendel was portrayed made him look like a hulking, hairless vampire, wading out of a lake of blood. But then, in the same book, the Lambton Worm was a giant earthworm wrapped around a tree! For some reason, to my young mind, King Hrothgar's warriors became Napoleonic era soldiers, but the story of the monster that slaughtered so many men to sate its insatiable appetite stayed with me.

In time, of course, I learned that the story came from an Anglo-Saxon poem inspired by the mythic age of the Scandinavian sagas, but this only made it more appealing. It has influenced my own work over the years, since long before I ever sat down to write *Beowulf Beastslayer* – there is a Grendel-like Fen Beast in my very first published book, the Fighting Fantasy adventure *Spellbreaker* – but if it hadn't been for Miller's monstrous encyclopaedia, I might not have written my own take on the first superhero story of English Literature.

*A Dictionary of Monsters and Mysterious Beasts*, like so many of the books that inspired me as a child and set me on the road to becoming an author, was given to me by my mother, and it is for this reason, as well as countless others, that this book is dedicated to her memory.

*Jill Mary Green*

*21st August 1935 – 22nd November 2018*

# BEOWULF
# BEASTSLAYER

# In the Land of the Danes

## "On land Dena"

### Introduction

The book you hold in your hands is a gateway to the world of the Scandinavian sagas, a time of bold heroes and dread monsters. Once inside its pages, you will find yourself travelling to King Hrothgar's golden hall of Heorot, to embark upon a thrilling epic of your own.

For this is no ordinary book. Rather than reading it from cover to cover, you will discover that at the end of each narrative section you will be presented with a series of choices that allow you to control the course of the story.

In *Beowulf Beastslayer* you will be transformed into the eponymous hero of the Anglo-Saxon epic poem, as you set sail with your fellow warriors to hunt down the monster Grendel and rid Heorot of its terrible curse. But on this occasion, you will decide which path to take, which risks to brave, and even which of the strange creatures and diabolical horrors you will encounter during your quest to engage in battle.

Success is by no means certain and you may well fail to complete the adventure at your first attempt. However, with experience, skill, and maybe even a little luck, each new attempt should bring you closer to your ultimate goal.

In addition to the book itself, you will need two six-sided dice, or a conventional pack of 52 playing cards, a pencil, an eraser, and a copy of the *Beowulf Beastslayer* Adventure Sheet (spare copies of which can be downloaded from www. acegamebooks.com).

# "An wīg gearwe"

## Playing the Game

There are three ways to play through *Beowulf Beastslayer*. The first is to use two conventional six-sided dice. The second is to use a conventional pack of 52 playing cards. The third is to ignore the rules altogether and just read the book, making choices as appropriate, but ignoring any combat or attribute tests, always assuming you win every battle and pass every skill test. (Even if you play the adventure this way, there is still no guarantee that you will complete it at your first attempt.)

If you are opting to play through *Beowulf Beastslayer* using the game rules, you first need to determine your strengths and weaknesses.

# "Eafoþes cræftig"

## Your Attributes

You have three attributes you will need to keep track of during the course of the adventure, using the Adventure Sheet. Some of these will change frequently, others less so, but it is important that you keep an accurate record of the current level for all of them.

*Agility* – This is a measure of how athletic and agile you are. If you need to leap across a chasm or dodge a deadly projectile, this is the attribute that will be employed.

*Combat* – This is a measure of how skilful you are at fighting, whether it be in unarmed combat, or wielding a keen-edged blade in battle.

*Endurance* – This is a measure of how physically tough you are and how much strength you have left. This attribute will vary more than any other during the course of your adventure.

Unlike some adventure gamebooks, in *Beowulf Beastslayer* your strengths and weaknesses are not determined randomly. Instead, you get to decide what you are good at, and, conversely, what you might not be so good at.

Your *Agility* and *Combat* attributes start at a base level of 6. Your *Endurance* score starts at a base level of 20. You then have a pool of 10 extra points to share out between *Agility, Combat* and *Endurance* as you see fit, but you can only add up to 5 points to each attribute. So the maximum starting score for *Agility* and *Combat* is 11, and the maximum starting score for *Endurance* is 25. (You must apportion all 10 points one way or another, and cannot leave any unused.)

For example, you might choose to add nothing to your *Agility* score, 5 points to your *Combat* score, and add the remaining 5 points to your *Endurance* score, making you a mighty warrior and giving you the following starting profile for the game:

*Agility* = 6, *Combat* = 11, *Endurance* = 25.

Alternatively, you might want to add 4 points to you *Agility* and *Combat* scores, and the remaining 2 points to your *Endurance* score, making you more of an all-rounder, and giving you this starting profile:

*Agility* = 10, *Combat* = 10, *Endurance* = 22.

Having determined where your strengths and weaknesses lie, record the value of each attribute in the appropriate box on the Adventure Sheet in pencil, and make sure you have an eraser to hand, as they will doubtless all change at some point as you play through the adventure (and some more than others).

There are limits on how high each of your attributes can be at the start of the adventure, but there are also limits on how high they can be raised during the course of the adventure, dependent upon bonus points you may be awarded. Neither your *Agility* score nor your *Combat* score may exceed 12 points, while your *Endurance* score may not exceed 30 points. However, should your *Endurance* score ever drop to zero, or below, then your adventure is over and you should stop

reading immediately; if you want to tackle the quest again, you will have to start from the beginning, determining your attributes anew, and then starting the story from section 1 once more.

# "Hæle hildedēor"

### Hero Points

In addition to your three basic attributes, you also have a pool of *Hero Points*. You start with 4 *Hero Points* but, during the course of your adventure, you can collect more by carrying out brave deeds and dramatic feats. However, you can also lose Hero Points by behaving in a way not befitting of a hero.

Throughout your adventure you will find that you will be able to 'spend' any *Hero Points* you have collected to help you overcome certain obstacles. For example, rather than Take an Agility test to see if you manage to leap across a chasm, you might spend some *Hero Points* to ensure that you make it across to the other side. Alternatively, you might spend some *Hero Points* to make sure you win a particular battle. How many *Hero Points* such actions cost will be stated in the text.

Please note that your *Hero Points* total may never drop below zero.

# "Ac hē mægnes rōf mīn costode"

### Testing Your Attributes

At various times during the adventure, you will be asked to test one or other of your attributes.

If it is your *Agility* or *Combat* that is being tested, simply roll two dice. If the total rolled is equal to or less than the particular attribute being tested, you have passed the test; if the total rolled is greater than the attribute in question, then you have failed the test.

If it is your *Endurance* score that is being tested, roll four dice in total. If the combined score of all four dice is equal to or less than your *Endurance* score, then you have passed the test, but if it is greater, then what is being asked of you is beyond you, and you have failed the test.

You may also be asked to roll against your *Hero Points* by taking a *Hero test*. If so, roll one die. If the total rolled is equal to or less than your total number of *Hero Points*, you have passed the test; if the total rolled is greater than your total number of *Hero Points*, then you have failed the test. However, having taken a *Hero test*, you must then deduct 1 *Hero Point* from your total.

# "Strenge getrūwode"

### Restoring Your Attributes

There are various ways that you can restore lost attribute points, or be granted bonuses that take your attributes beyond their starting scores, and these will be described in the text.

However, an easy way to restore lost *Endurance* points is to find sustenance. Sometimes you may find enough sustenance that you can take some with you to consume later on in the adventure.

Make sure that if you do find any supplies of this nature you record them in the Meals box on your Adventure Sheet, along with any information about exactly how many attribute points they will restore when consumed. (Unless you are told otherwise by the text, one Meal will restore 4 *Endurance* points.)

You start your adventure without any Meals.

# "Grim gūð"

## Combat

You will repeatedly be called upon to defend yourself against the creatures and monsters that dwell upon the misty fells and within the wild fenlands. Sometimes you may even choose to attack these horrors yourself. After all, as they say, the best form of defence is attack.

When this happens, start by filling in your opponent's Combat and Endurance scores in the first available Beowulf Encounter Box on your Adventure Sheet.

Whenever you engage in combat, you will be told in the text whether you or your enemy has the initiative; in other words, who has the advantage and gets to attack first.

1. Roll two dice and add your *Combat* score. The resulting total is your *Combat Rating*.

2. Roll two dice and add your opponent's *Combat* score. The resulting total is your opponent's *Combat Rating*.

3. For each Combat Round, add a temporary 1 point bonus to the *Combat Rating* of whichever of the combatants has the initiative for the duration of that round.

4. If your *Combat Rating* is higher than your opponent's you have wounded your enemy; deduct 2 points from your opponent's *Endurance* score, and move on to step 7.

5. If your opponent's *Combat Rating* is higher, then you have been wounded; deduct 2 points from your *Endurance* score, and move on to step 8.

6. If your *Combat Rating* and your opponent's *Combat Rating* are the same, roll one die. If the number rolled is odd, you and your opponent deflect each other's attacks; go to step 10. If the number rolled is even, go to step 9.

7.  If your opponent's *Endurance* score has been reduced to zero or below, you have won; the battle is over and you can continue on your way. If your opponent is not yet dead, go to step 10.

8.  If your *Endurance* score has been reduced to zero or below, your opponent has won the battle. If you want to continue your adventure you will have to start again from the beginning, determining your attributes anew. However, if you are still alive, go to step 10.

9.  You and your opponent have both managed to injure each other; deduct 1 point from both your *Endurance* score and your opponent's *Endurance* score. If your *Endurance* score has been reduced to zero or below, your adventure is over; if you want to play again you will have to start again from the beginning. If you are still alive but your enemy's *Endurance* has been reduced to zero or below, you have won; the battle is over and you can continue on your way. If neither you nor your opponent is dead, go to step 10.

10. If you won the Combat Round, you will have the initiative in the next Combat Round. If your opponent won the Combat Round, they will have the initiative. If neither of you won the Combat Round, neither of you will gain the initiative bonus for the next Combat Round. Go back to step 1 and work through the sequence again until either your opponent is dead, or you are defeated.

Occasionally you may find yourself having to fight more than one opponent at once. Such battles are conducted in the same way as above, using the ten-step process, except that you will have to work out the *Combat Ratings* of all those involved. As long as you have a higher rating than an opponent you will injure them, no matter how many opponents you are taking on at the same time. However, equally, any opponent with a *Combat Rating* higher than yours will be able to injure you too.

# "Wīgspēda gewiofu"

## An Alternative to Dice

Rather than rolling dice, you may prefer to determine random numbers during the game using a pack of playing cards.

To do this, when you are called upon to roll dice, simply shuffle a standard 52-card deck (having removed the jokers) and draw a single card. (If you are asked to roll four dice, draw two cards.) Number cards are worth the number shown on the card. Jacks, Queens and Kings are all worth 11, and if you draw an Ace, it counts as being worth 12 (for example, if you are engaged in Combat), and is an automatic pass if you are testing an attribute – any attribute.

After drawing from the deck you can either return any cards you have drawn or, using the Pontoon method, leave those drawn cards out of the deck. Both styles of play will influence how lucky, or unlucky, you may be during the game, when it comes to determining random numbers.

# "Gūðsearo geatolīc"

## Equipment

You start your adventure with a sword, a shield, a spear, a shirt of chainmail, and a war-helm. During the course of your quest you will no doubt acquire all manner of other items that may be of use to you later on. Anything that you do collect should be recorded on your Adventure Sheet, including weapons, meals, and other miscellaneous objects.

# "Eorlweorod"

## Crew

You do not travel to the land of the Danes alone, but are accompanied by your own fighting-band of Geatish storm-warriors. Your company, not including yourself, starts out at 14. Record this total in the *Crew* box on your Adventure Sheet.

## "Swutol sang scopes"

### Kennings

As you forge the legend of *Beowulf Beastslayer*, you will doubtless be asked to record various kennings on your Adventure Sheet. Make sure you do so, as these will help to track what you have or haven't done during the course of your adventure.

## "Ic þis gid be þē āwræc wintrum frōd"

### Hints on Play

There is more than one path that you can follow through *Beowulf Beastslayer* to reach your ultimate goal, but it may take you several attempts to actually complete the adventure. Make notes and draw a map as you explore. This map will doubtless prove invaluable during future attempts at completing the quest, and will allow you to progress more speedily in order to reach unexplored regions.

Keep a careful eye on all of your attributes throughout the game. Beware of traps and setting off on wild goose chases. However, it would be wise to collect useful items along the way that may aid you further on in your quest.

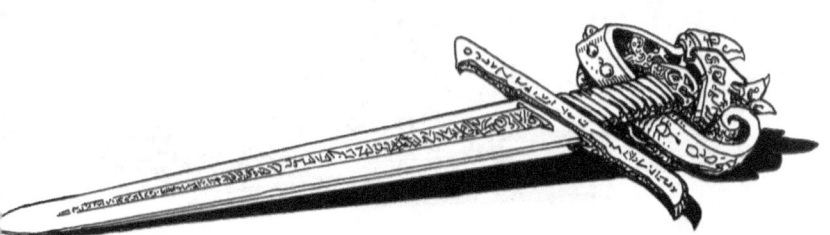

# "Endestæf"

## Ending the Game

There are several ways that your adventure can end. If your *Endurance* score ever drops to zero or below, your trials have exhausted and overcome you. If this happens, stop reading at once.

There may also be occasions where you are prevented from progressing any further through the adventure thanks to the choices you have made, or if you meet a sudden and untimely end. In all of these cases, if you want to have another crack at completing the adventure you will have to start again with a new Adventure Sheet and begin the story afresh from the beginning.

There is of course one other reason for your adventure coming to an end, and that is if you successfully complete your quest, the very same quest that awaits you now...

# BEOWULF BEASTSLAYER
## ADVENTURE SHEET

AGILITY

MEALS

COMBAT

CREW

ENDURANCE

HERO POINTS

EQUIPMENT

KENNINGS

# BEOWULF
## ENCOUNTERS BOXES

COMBAT=
ENDURANCE=

COMBAT=
ENDURANCE=

COMBAT=
ENDURANCE=

COMBAT=
ENDURANCE=

COMBAT=
ENDURANCE=

COMBAT=
ENDURANCE=

COMBAT=
ENDURANCE=

COMBAT=
ENDURANCE=

COMBAT=
ENDURANCE=

COMBAT=
ENDURANCE=

# BEOWULF
## ENCOUNTERS BOXES

COMBAT=
ENDURANCE=

COMBAT=
ENDURANCE=

COMBAT=
ENDURANCE=

COMBAT=
ENDURANCE=

COMBAT=
ENDURANCE=

COMBAT=
ENDURANCE=

COMBAT=
ENDURANCE=

COMBAT=
ENDURANCE=

COMBAT=
ENDURANCE=

COMBAT=
ENDURANCE=

# Hwæt!

# King Hrothgar's Curse

Hear, and listen well, my friends, and I shall tell you a tale that has been told a thousand thousand times before, for a thousand years and more.

This saga begins when Hrothgar – son of Healfdane, son of Beow, son of Scyld – was king of the Spear-Danes. Indeed, he was the mightiest warrior-chieftain that land had seen since Scyld Scefing; he who had raised Denmark out of darkness, uniting its noble lords.

Fierce in battle, Hrothgar brought home more treasure from his conquests than any ring-giver before him. And he decreed that a mead-hall should be raised, the like of which had never been seen under heaven, and named it Heorot.

But in the borderlands that bound the lands of the Danes there dwelt a hell-fiend, a hater of mirth, to whom the song of the skald was as the shrieking of the night-owl, or the scream of the vixen, a ghastly grinder of bones, the marsh-monster Grendel. And in his fen-fell fastness, this spawn of evil devised all manner of blood-thirsty atrocities that he would bring down upon the Dane-folk to exact his revenge against them.

When night fell on Hrothgar's high house, the dark-dweller crept from his cave and came to gold-gabled Heorot, and there found the noble company slumbering after the feast. Those proud warriors did not know sorrow until that damned troll-born demon-progeny, grim and greedy, savage and cruel, burst into the hall and seized in their sleep thirty thanes. With his perditious plunder in his gory grasp, the monster slunk back to the hole whence he had crawled, and there banqueted upon the bodies.

As the fair jewel of heaven banished the darkness once more, the next morning Grendel's grievous maiming-might was revealed to Hrothgar and his company, and proud feast-boasts gave way to wailing lamentations.

The very next night, the grisly ghoul came to the high-antlered hall, and there perpetrated savage slaughter against the host of Heorot once more, stealing away another twenty souls to sate his gluttonous greed.

The mighty chieftain sat in sorrow, suffering the anguish of his thanes' deaths.

Consumed now by viciousness and violence, the night-stalker would not be appeased. And so the greatest of feast-halls fell silent and stood empty, no longer a monument to mirth and merriment, but a memorial to murder and misery.

For twelve long years the bitter blood-feud continued until one day, from across the sea, came the one called Beowulf.

The Bee-Wolf. The Bear. The Beastslayer.

Now turn to **1**.

## 1

Urged by the wind, *Sea-Wolf*, the well-braced wave-cutter, skims over the swan's riding. Wind-whetted and white-throated, the curved prow ploughs the sea hard, while the harnessed warriors of the Geats – the Storm-folk, resplendent in their bright mail-coats, their war-gear well-wrought – pull hard on the oars, at your command.

A day out from home, the sky grows night-black and with storm-wrought waves rising like dark mountains about the ship, your men begin to tire and falter in their stroke.

"Good men of Geatland, proud subjects of King Hygelac," you exhort your warrior-band, "you fourteen are the fiercest warriors of the fiercest warrior-folk in this middle-earth! Row hard for today is not your decreed death-day!"

"Stroke! Stroke!" you shout, the shout becoming a chant as you seek to help your men row in time with one another. But do you have the skill to keep the rowers together?

If you want to ensure that your rhythmic chanting keeps your men in time, deduct 1 *Hero Point* and turn to **31**.

If not, *Take an Agility test*; if you pass the test, turn to **31**, but if you fail the test, turn to **61**.

## 2

As the Dragon's fiery venom takes hold, burning through your blood-stream, so the talisman grows warm against your skin, the magic imbued within it working with your body's own constitution to expunge the poison from your veins.

If you have Thor's Favour or Loki's Favour, recorded on your Adventure Sheet, turn to **500**.

If not, *Take an Endurance test*. If you pass the test, turn to **500**, but if you fail the test, turn to **380**.

Alternatively, you may spend 1 *Hero Point* and turn to **500** automatically.

### 3

"What do you want?" challenges one of the ogres, stepping forward from the ranks of its tribe. "Do you fancy your chances too?"

"Never mind what he wants," growls another, "let's just kill 'im and eat 'im, like we did with the others."

"No, this one's up to something," says the first. "I can see it in 'is eyes. What are you up to?"

"I was just thinking how easy it would be to kill you all without even having to lift my little finger," you tell the giant, a wry smile on your face.

"What do you mean?" the giant replies and then starts to roar with laughter. "A wee scrag of a thing like you, kill a whole tribe o' giants like us?"

His fellows join him in his expression of mirth.

"As easily as I could crush a flower in the palm of my hand."

"We'll see about that," snarls the giant, hefting its great stone club in its misshapen hands.

You casually point at one of the other giants with your sword. "Especially after I heard him say how you're the weakest giant in the Orkneys."

Roll one die (or pick a card). If the number rolled is odd (or the card is red), turn to **20**. If the number rolled is even (or the card is black), turn to **120**.

Alternatively, if you are able to, you may spend 1 *Hero Point* to invoke your heroic status by turning to **120**.

## 4

Are you wearing your chainmail war-shirt? If so, turn to **362**, but if not, turn to **302**.

## 5

Giving a parched battle-cry, the deathless guardian leaps at you, its sword raised.

If you have The Lord's Favour recorded on your Adventure Sheet, turn to **35**. If not, turn to **57**.

## 6

As Nótt spreads her dusk-dark mantle over the world, you and your men creep from your hiding place at the edge of the hills and advance upon King Hrothgar's hall.

Although the darkness hides your approach from the night-blind eyes of the sentries, it cannot hide the ripe smell of you from the slavering, snarl-mouthed dogs that guard the palisade surrounding Heorot.

As the hounds threaten to summon the night-stalker himself with their barking, you and your men hasten to silence them. It is at that moment one Wolfhound slips its tether and leaps at you. (In this battle the Wolfhound has the initiative.)

WOLFHOUND          COMBAT 6       ENDURANCE 6

If you want to guarantee that you win the fight with the guard dog, deduct 1 *Hero Point* and turn to **109**. If not, you will have to defend yourself against the animal, and only turn to **109** if you win.

The rich flesh of the deer is moist and succulent. Not only that but, as well as the stag being the animal-spirit of kingship, deer carry within them the power to heal.

Gain 3 *Endurance* points and 1 *Agility* point.

Turn to **390**.

The un-dead warriors raise their ancient, tarnished blades and engage you in combat.

(In this battle, the draugr have the initiative, and you must fight them both at the same time.)

|  | COMBAT | ENDURANCE |
|---|---|---|
| First DRAUGR THANE | 9 | 8 |
| Second DRAUGR THANE | 8 | 8 |

If you wish, you may spend 2 *Hero Points* to automatically win this battle (turn to **150**).

If not, conduct the battle as normal and, if you defeat both your opponents, turn to **150**.

## 9

As you pray, sleep takes you and you dream of Freya, whose beauty is as radiant as the sun. You beseech her to watch over you in her beneficence, and guard you from all ills that those cursed with sin-born ugliness would visit upon you.

Record Freya's Favour on your Adventure Sheet and then turn to **427**.

## 10

The monster sinks back into the chill embrace of the deep ocean. And then, through the rain and tumultuous waves, a smudge of land on the skyline becomes the shimmer of sea-cliffs and wave-washed rocks, sheer fells rising into mist beyond.

The crossing is at an end – turn to **60**.

## 11

You are Sigurd, son of Sigmund and Last of the Völsungs, a warrior of Denmark. After Reginn the Dvergr forged the sword Gram for you, you assembled an army of warriors and took to the whale-road with them, sailing to the sovereign lands of King Lyngvi. A series of bloody battles followed, in which you avenged your father's death and put an end to an ancient blood-feud, by striking down all your foes and winning great renown. You finally returned to Denmark, a true blooded warrior.

(Gain 3 *Endurance* points, 1 *Combat* point, and 1 *Agility* point.)

Soon after your return, Reginn came to you and reminded you of your promise to slay Fáfnir. And so, the very next day, the two of you rode out together – man and dwarf – in search of the wyrm.

\*　\*　\*　\*

Day after day, Reginn leads you through empty lands where no one dwells, until finally you come to a lonely heath. There you spy a track, formed of withered plants and worn earth, that leads to a stinking stagnant pool. The track is wide and the extent of the blackened grass and withered plants causes you to wonder as to the size of the beast that made it, thoughts you express to Reginn.

"Do not fear," the dwarf says. "Dig a pit in the ground and wait within, until the wyrm passes over you. Then you can attack from underneath."

However, having proposed such a plan, Reginn rides off to find somewhere to hide.

If you want to start digging, as the dwarf suggested, turn to **92**. If you would prefer to find somewhere else to hide, while you wait for the wrym to appear, turn to **75**.

### 12

"Twelve years that demon-monster has tormented your people, if the skalds have it right," you reply.

"I regret to report that the song-weavers do indeed speak the truth," says the other sorrowfully. "But it warms my heart to know that an ally of old has come to save us."

Gain 1 *Hero Point*, add the kenning *Dane-Friend* to your Adventure Sheet, and then turn to **34**.

Deeper and deeper you go, the pressure in your lungs building all the time, until you can hold your breath no longer. As the ogress squeezes your body close to her hideous wrinkled form, you open your mouth and the air bursts from your mouth in a rush of bubbles. Freezing water fills your lungs and you are dead before the hag sinks her fangs into you and starts to feast.

Your adventure is over.

# THE END

Leaving the chapel behind, you and your brave warriors ride on.

Crossing the moors, where the gorse and bilberry bushes have been burnt by the serpent's rage, you come to a place that was once a forest, before the Dragon's ire stripped the trees of their leaves and left them as stark black monuments to their former glory.

And then the dragon takes flight once again, sensing your presence within the bounds of its dominions, and seeking to rid itself of such an irritation. At its coming, your band of hand-picked companions, faint of heart in the presence of the monster-serpent, do not stand as battle-usage expects, but escape to the withered wood. All but one.

Faithful Wiglaf remains at your side as the dragon hunts those that have fled from you through the burnt forest. The cowardly oath-breakers dead, roasted by the serpent's tongues of flame before being devoured by the creature, the worm returns to its cave to sleep.

The only ones among your hunting party left alive, you and Wiglaf make your way to the mound of earth wherein the guardian and its hoard have lain for so many generations, unmolested.

The bonds of kinship are strong between you, for Wiglaf is Weoxstan's son, well-loved shieldsman and Scylfing prince, but it is for this reason that you cannot bear to see him, another of your kinsmen, fall to the wrath of this Ravager.

"The burden of this battle lies upon my shoulders," you tell Wiglaf. "It is only my mind's-worth that needs be tested this day."

"As a Geatish prince of your hall, I have sworn blood-oaths to you, King Beowulf. My life is yours to do with as you will," is Wiglaf's response.

"I do not fear for my own life," you impress upon him. "Battles aplenty have I survived, and valiant in all dangers have I come through many clashes since the cleansing of bright Heorot. But I would not have another risk himself in battle against this fell hall-burner."

"Forgive me, my lord, but I see how this worm torments you, and recalling the many favours you have bestowed upon me – the rich dwelling-place of the Waymundings, confirming me as holder of the land-rights my father once held – I would be nothing without you. To stand by your side now, at the time of your greatest need, would be as sweet to me as the mead served in your royal hall."

Will you give in, and let Wiglaf accompany you into the barrow (turn to **40**), or will you stand firm and deny him his wish (turn to **74**)?

## 15

The killer-fish drags your soul-fled corpse to the bottom of the black ocean and there begins to devour it, limb by limb, piece by piece…

Turn to **308**.

## 16

The water is filled with squeaking shrieking noises as the nicors turn tail and disappear ahead of you along the tunnel. Taking this as a good sign, and making the most of the opportunity this provides, you follow, hoping that they might lead you to their dam.

Turn to **81**.

## 17

You find yourself within a great grey vault beneath the earth, its roof supported by stone arches anchored on pillars, and you lay eyes upon that underground hall heaped with a dead king's glory, that ancient wealth, that golden inheritance, that serpent-geld.

*Take an Agility test.* If you pass the test, turn to **121**, but if you fail the test, turn to **193**.

Alternatively, you may spend 1 *Hero Point* to avoid having to take the test at all, and turn to **121** straightaway.

## 18

Trapped in the death-shark's jaws, you struggle to fight your way free and fail. The crushing depths force the air from your lungs and you drown before the hunter can devour you…

Turn to **308**.

## 19

A number of the King's men have put their trust in spears rather than swords and half a dozen of them hurl their war-shafts at you.

*Take an Agility test.* If you pass the test, turn to **68**, but if you fail the test, turn to **130**.

"Oh aye? Well we'll see about that!" the giant snarls.

Hefting its great club in its misshapen hands, the brute charges towards you at a lumbering run. (In this battle the giant has the initiative.)

ELADA THE ETTIN          COMBAT 6          ENDURANCE 9

If you want to, you may spend 1 *Hero Point* to automatically win your battle against the giant (turn to **49**).

If not, conduct the battle as normal and, if you win, turn to **49**. However, if you lose, turn to **79**.

The monster's tentacles slip from about the boat and sink back into the sea, which is now boiling with blood and black ink, as the Kraken retreats to its lightless lair at the bottom of the Jormungandr's domain.

Turn to **36**.

Against all the odds, you make it to the cave-mouth in the cliff-face. Your grip tight on your war-tooth, you pass from the icy wind and freezing sea-spray into the chill darkness of the Dragon's lair, alone.

Turn to **388**.

## 23

"I wrestled the monster Grendel, who haunted the hall of King Hrothgar of Denmark, and tore off his arm with my bare hands," you tell the King, "and then I entered the lake-lair of his hag-mother and took her head too. And so I believe I can slay this fire-breathing tormentor."

Gain 1 *Hero Point*.

"A bold claim!" declares the king. "But a would-be dragon-slayer needs a dragon-slaying sword, and so I offer you mine to use in the coming battle."

If you want to accept the Draugr King's unexpected gift, turn to **43**. If you would prefer to politely decline, turn to **105**.

## 24

The Norns must be looking kindly upon your endeavours this night, for you to have escaped being injured by the Varulfur at all.

Gain 2 *Hero Points* and turn to **342**.

## 25

The mead-horn having gone round more than once during their feast, you find Hrothgar's karls asleep, snoring their drunkenness to the rafters.

At your arrival they begin to stir, but before they can gather their wits, maddened with rage, you strike quickly and with utter ruthlessness.

Catching them up in your cruel claws, you hurl six of the sleeping warriors against the walls of the hall, dashing their brains out against the sturdy wooden pillars.

Make a note that you have dealt with 6 men, and then turn to **347**.

Transfixed by the horror of it all, you act too slowly to defend yourself as Grendel's corpse lashes out with its intact hand, raking your arms with its talons. (Lose 3 *Endurance* points.)

Shaken from your reverie, in single-minded anger you intend to settle with the monster for those stealthy raids it made on Hrothgar's people, using the steel still in your hands. (Grendel has the initiative in this battle.)

GRENDEL                          COMBAT 8          ENDURANCE 9

If you wish you may spend 1 *Hero Point* to automatically win your battle with the risen Grendel (turn to **191**). If not conduct the battle as normal and, if you win, turn to **191**.

Your warriors fight the waves with oars, not swords, their enemy the ocean-sound, as the *Sea-Wolf* rides out the storm beneath black-cliff walls of water. And as the Geats beat back the sea-surges with their blades of wood, something finds you, out in the cold ocean.

Sea hunter. Wave rider. Black fish. Killer whale.

Its tall black fin rises from amidst the waves like the sail of a death-ship. And then the hump of its back breaks the surface and you feel the blood-quickening thrill of the chase.

Will you arm yourself and make your way to the stern, ready to fight off this monster of the black brine (make a note that you have the initiative and turn to **217**), or will you compel your men to propel the *Sea-Wolf* away from the black-finned hunter (turn to **140**)?

## 28

The un-dead warriors raise their ancient, tarnished blades and engage the two of you in battle.

As Wiglaf engages the first of them, you tackle the second. (In this battle, the draugr has the initiative.)

| | | |
|---|---|---|
| DRAUGR THANE | COMBAT 8 | ENDURANCE 8 |

If you wish, you may spend 1 *Hero Point* to automatically win this battle (turn to **150**).

If not, conduct the battle as normal and, if you defeat your opponent, then turn to **150**.

## 29

A feeling of abject fear falls over you like a shroud, and you start to doubt your ability to defeat the giants. And it is not only you who is feeling like this now; you can see that your men are quailing and quaking in fear too!

The giant tribe's druid has damned you all with its curse-spell. (Lose 1 *Hero Point*.)

There is only one way to shatter the charm and that is to slay the charm-weaver. Summoning what little courage you have left, you make your move against the druid, as another of the ogres hurries to the soothsayer's defence.

You must fight the giants at the same time, and in this battle your opponents have the initiative.

| | COMBAT | ENDURANCE |
|---|---|---|
| DAGDA THE DRUID | 7 | 10 |
| CROM THE CROOKED | 8 | 11 |

If you somehow manage to slay both the giants, turn to **465**, but if you lose the battle, turn to **79**.

The King accepts the proffered purse. (Cross the Purse of Ancient Coins off your Adventure Sheet.)

"I suppose that will suffice," the draugr says, having taken a moment to count the money. "But tell me, who are you and why have you really invaded my earthen hall?"

You see no reason to lie to the un-dead lord of this place and so begin to relate your story.

"I am King Beowulf, of the hardy Storm-folk of Geatland. A knavish slave stole this cup from your treasure-store," you say, holding up the Golden Goblet, "and in doing so, disturbed the Dragon that has laid claim to your ancient hoard."

"What?" roars the King. "A scale-skinned fire-breather has taken my treasure-hoard?"

"Yes, O King," you reply, "and I have come to slay it."

"It pleases my ear to hear such noble sentiment," says the King, mellowing, "but what makes you think you are capable of completing such a task?"

And so you begin to list your mighty feats and great accomplishments, any one of your myriad victories worthy of being a proud hero's mead-hall boast. But are they enough to convince the King?

During the course of your adventure, you may have already related tales of past deeds, or even listened to the sagas of other heroes. If so, you will have a number associated with each story. If you have three such numbers, arrange them in the order you acquired them to create a three-digit number, divide that number by 2, and then turn to the section which has the same number as the final total. If not, turn to **23**.

You keep the rowers' rhythm strong and the *Sea-Wolf's* course straight and true, until wind and waves relent.

On only the second day out from Geatland, you catch sight of land looming on the skyline. You see the shimmer of cliffs, and sheer fells behind, while your men cheer for "Brave Beowulf!" and "Noble Beowulf!" and "Sea-wise Beowulf!"

Your voyage is at an end.

Turn to **60**.

**32**

Safely on the other side, realising that you cannot be far from the hoard-hall of the serpent-king, you consider how best to prepare yourself for the confrontation to come.

Now would be a good time to eat some provisions or imbibe a healing balm. You must also decide which sword you want to use to fight the Dragon, as you will not be able to change weapons in the heat of battle.

Once you have made your choice and readied yourself, turn to **411**.

## 33

Conclude your battle with the Dragon, using the stats you have recorded for the worm on your Adventure Sheet.

If you manage to reduce its *Endurance* score to 6 points or fewer, or after another four Combat Rounds (whichever is sooner), turn to **176**.

If you wish, you may spend 1 *Hero Point* and turn to **176** straightaway instead.

## 34

"I believe you are a man of your word," the look-out says, "so I will bring you to Heorot and Hrothgar, Protector of the Scyldings."

And so you set off, your warriors – clad in their chainmail shirts, with long ashen spears in their hands, as well as their mighty war-shields – briskly marching together as you follow the Coast Warden, their boar-helms gleaming in the sunlight, now that the storm has passed.

Turn to **232**.

## 35

Whenever you find yourself in battle against one or more of the dead-walking draugr, such as now, you may add 1 point when calculating your *Combat Rating* for the duration of that battle.

Now turn to **57**.

Your ship's ring-bound prow planing the waters, on the second day after leaving the Land of the Danes, you catch sight of the cliffs and headlands you know so well. The hull of the *Sea-Wolf* drives ahead, urged by the breeze, and beaches on the shore.

The harbour-guard is waiting at the water's edge – having scoured the stretches of the great sea-flood ever since you left, hoping to one day espy the returning host of heroes – and now he moors your broad-ribbed boat in the sand, held fast with hawsers so no heft of the waves should drive that trusted vessel to the flood once more. He has your heroes' hoard brought ashore, while you go to meet your long-missed lord, Hygelac, at the hall where he dwells with his own hero-band, hard by the sea-wall.

It is a handsome hall, but nothing like Hrothgar's gold-gabled Heorot. High within it sits King Hygelac, son of Hrethel, and a warrior of great courage, with his consort, Queen Hygd.

The news of your return has already reached the chieftain-king: the Shield of Warriors, his own battle-companion Beowulf, has returned from Hrothgar's kingdom, alive and feted, as a noble hero should be.

Hygelac welcomes you warmly, a feast is prepared, and you sit facing the King, kinsman to kinsman, while Hygd carries the mead-horn about the hall, presenting it to each of your storm-warriors in turn. Curiosity burning within him, Hygelac presses you to tell him of your adventures in the Land of the Spear-Danes.

And so you tell your lord of your battle with the arch-fiend Grendel, and – after the monster's mother sought revenge for her son being death-taken by Geat war-spite – how you penetrated the monster's lair, there to slay Grendel's dam, while the world's candle sinks below the sea-horizon to the west.

Your tale concluded, you tell your uncle-king, "The Lord of the Scyldings bestowed upon me many treasures, which now, brave king, I give to you. Joy, for me, lies in the giving, and I have little family in the world, Hygelac, beside yourself."

You bid the harbour-guard bring in all the gifts the generous ring-giver Hrothgar gave to you.

And Hygelac rewards you just as richly. He lays a royal sword – bright-gleaming Naegling – in your lap, and bestows upon you an estate of seven thousand hides, a chief's stool and a hall of your own.

Add the sword Naegling to your Equipment List and then turn to **310**.


## 37

The warrior has you fast by the arm now and will not let go. You twist and turn, fighting to break free of his astonishingly powerful grasp.

*Take and Endurance test.* If you pass the test, turn to **142**, but if you fail the test, turn to **494**.


## 38

The ferocity and strength of the wild boar make such animals worthy adversaries for the hunt, and the prize, when the battle with the beast is won, is a meat that is rich and delicious, and one that imparts part of the boar's fighting-frenzy into the one who dines upon it.

Gain 4 *Endurance* points and 1 *Combat* point.

Turn to **390**.

## 39

Twisting and turning, clasped as you are within the death-shark's jaws, you manage to wrestle your sword-arm free. With a powerful thrust you plunge the tip of your blade into the monster's eye.

Giving a silent-scream, the hakarl releases its hold on you. In that moment, with a powerful kick of your legs you push yourself clear of its mouth. But then, in its blind rage, the fish goes for you again.

You are ready for it this time. Your sword finds the pale flesh of its belly, and pulling hard on your blade, you gut the monster-fish with one stroke.

Turn to **90**.

## 40

Relenting at last, you give Wiglaf permission to join you in entering the Dragon's earthen hall.

"Beloved Beowulf," the young prince says, "bear all things well! You gave it out long ago that, living, you would not allow your glory to ever abate. Bold-tempered chieftain, you who are famed for your deeds, you must defend now your own life with all your strength. And I shall aid you."

Write the kenning *Shield-Prince* on your Adventure Sheet and make a note that if you should ever come across a section number with the symbol of a helmet beneath it, rather than read that section, add 20 and turn to this new section instead, before proceeding.

Now turn to **74**.

"King!" you declare, your voice echoing from the granite slab.

As the echo fades, you hear an almost imperceptible click and the huge stone door swings open.

Turn to **423**.

Against all the odds, you make it to the cave-mouth in the cliff-face. Wiglaf makes the descent as well and joins you there, at the entrance to the cave.

Swords in hand, you pass from the icy wind and freezing sea-spray into the chill darkness of the Dragon's lair, together.

Turn to **388**.

Taking the corpse-king's sword, you marvel at the skill of the weapon-smith who forged it in ages past. The surface of the blade is tarnished with corrosion, but its edge is still keen, even after all these centuries.

But there is something else. Reading the runes etched into the blade you realise that this is the legendary Angurvadal, the Stream of Anguish, a sword passed down from generation to generation, from a forgotten age of myths and legends.

Add Angurvadal to your Equipment List, gain 2 *Hero Points*, and then turn to **105**.

Jaws gaping, the nicors attack together. (In this battle, the nicors have the initiative.)

NICORS                    COMBAT 7        ENDURANCE 7

If you wish, you may spend 1 *Hero Point* to automatically win your battle with the Nicors (turn to **63**).

If you do not wish to spend any *Hero Points*, you will have to conduct the battle as normal, except that while you are fighting the nicors, because you are doing so underwater, you must temporarily reduce your *Combat* score by 1 point. Also, because you are having to conduct this battle whilst holding your breath, if the battle lasts for more Combat Rounds than your current *Endurance* score, you will drown. If you defeat the fish-spawn, turn to **63**.

**45**

Lying inside the chest is a rotted leather bag, from which have spilled a mass of gold coins. You do not recognise the kingly image struck into them, and cannot quite decode the runes that ring the regal face.

Do you want to take the treasure? If so, turn to **88**. If you think it better to leave the gold where it is, turn to **250**.

**46**

You are met at the gates of Heorot by a nobleman and a contingent of armed men.

"Who are you that you come to our gates bearing battle-brave arms and war-marked shields?" the noble demands, the tongue of metal that is his sword gripped tightly in his hand.

"I am Beowulf," you reply, tightening the grip on your own sword, "prince of the Geats, kin of King Hygelac, and I seek an audience with your king, Hrothgar."

Turn to **391**.

## 47

The rock finds its mark, hitting the giant in the middle of its forehead, and stays there. As dark blood begins to ooze from around the embedded boulder, the ogre's eyes roll up into its head and it topples to the ground like a felled tree.

Turn to **49**.

## 48

Making your way back through the network of caves you come to the chamber that has become the warrior's ill-deserved tomb.

At once, the same glow that greeted you before fills the narrow cave and the warrior's spirit-form appears before you. As you present the axe and the brooch, laying them on the ground beside his mortal remains, a smile forms on the phantom's lips.

"Thank you," comes the ghost's echoing voice. "You are truly a noble warrior. There is little I can give you in return for reuniting me with my possessions, other than to share the knowledge and experience I gained in life.

"While dining upon the meat of the deer will bestow a measure of the animal's agility upon a noble soul, and the flesh of the boar will impart a portion of the truffle-hunter's ferocity, the humble salmon offers the greatest reward, for eating of it can grant a man knowledge. And now I bid you farewell, brave Beowulf."

With that, the ghost fades into the shadows and is gone.

Turn to **395**.

## 49

As their brother falls, the other giants take a step back and exchange uncomfortable glances.

And then one of them – wearing a hooded robe stitched together from deer hides and carrying a driftwood staff – steps forward. The giant is muttering under its breath as it traces patterns in the air with the root-bole head of its bark-clean staff.

The giant is weaving a charm!

*Take a Hero test*. If you pass the test, turn to **485**. If you fail the test, turn to **29**.

## 50

It is time to finish the serpent-scaled fire-breather!

If you have Odin's Favour recorded on your Adventure Sheet, turn to **176**. If not, turn to **33**.

## 51

"Glámr!" you say, stating the name of the ancient king who lies sleeping within the barrow.

You hear an almost imperceptible click and the huge stone door swings open.

Turn to **423**.

## 52

Wiglaf joins you, safe on the other side.

"We cannot be far from the hoard-hall of that murder-glutton serpent-king," he says, his hushed voice still seeming uncomfortably loud as it echoes from the walls of the cave-tunnel.

"Then we must prepare ourselves for the battle to come," you reply.

Now would be a good time to eat some provisions. Wiglaf has a flask of Ypocras, a spiced wine infused with herbs, which acts as a powerful restorative, which he shares with you. (Gain 3 *Endurance* points, 1 *Combat* point, 1 *Agility* point, and 1 *Hero Point*.)

You must also decide which sword you want to use to challenge the dragon, as you will not be able to change weapons during the battle.

Once you have made your choice and readied yourself, turn to **411**.

## 53

As you pray, sleep takes you and you dream of Tyr, sacrificing his arm to Fenrir, the Wolf of the End Times, so that his brother gods might bind the monster to the earth.

You realise that to be the master of war you have to be prepared to make the ultimate sacrifice.

Record Tyr's Favour on your Adventure Sheet, add 1 point to your *Combat* score, and then turn to **427**.

## 54

The blood-thirsty skin-changer is dead. As you stare at its corpse, it starts to twist and change again, until you are looking at a naked man, his organs opened to the elements by your cruel sword-cuts.

If the Varulfur wounded you even once during your battle, turn to **4**. If the creature did not wound you at all, turn to **24**.

## 55

Before your eyes, Grendel's body rises from the plinth upon which it had been laid. The monster's eyes burn with hatred for the living, and a viscous slime oozes from the gaping wound in its shoulder.

To look upon the creature, from the pallid hue of its flesh to the life-ending wound you dealt it, you would think it a corpse, were it not for the fact that it is now stalking towards you, murderous intent twisting its horrifying face into a rictus of homicidal hatred.

*Take a Hero test.* If you pass the test, turn to **101**. If you fail the test, turn to **26**.

And so you come to King Hrothgar's cursed hall once more, but will you enter through the double doors, by which you gained egress last night (turn to **106**), or will you smash your way in through the wall (turn to **353**)?

**57**

You are startled by how quickly the creature can move, considering that it is a corpse! (In this battle, the draugr has the initiative.)

DRAUGR GUARD            COMBAT 8        ENDURANCE 7

If you wish, you may spend 1 *Hero Point* to automatically win this battle (turn to **99**).

If not, conduct combat as normal and, if you win, then turn to **99**.

**58**

Steadily the night's darkness grows and King Hrothgar's bodyguards rise to escort their leader, the grey-haired Scylding, from the hall. And you are ready to go to your bed too, after the day's exertions, brave bondsman that you are.

Fight-wearied, you take your rest, Hrothgar ensuring that all your wants – such as might be required of a sea-faring warrior – are provided for. This night you sleep within the wide-gabled hall until raven's-crow comes, as dawn gilds the sky.

With Heorot's curse lifted, you desire to see your homeland again. You and your storm-warriors rise with the sun, eager to set off, wishing to forge far in your ship.

When your company is prepared, your fighting-men armed and ready for the journey, you quit the hall and make your way to the stony beach where the *Sea-Wolf* lies waiting and renewed. Your spirited warrior-band is graciously greeted by the coast-warden. As he rides down from the cliff-top to meet them, he declares how pleased the Storm-folk will be to see the brave warriors return again in their shining armour.

As you are preparing to set sail, the lord of this land rides down to the shore on his gold-bridled steed. And you, Beowulf Beastslayer, the Joy of the Danes, hail the grey-haired king.

"In your hall we were royally treated, and you, noble Hrothgar, have entertained us well. But we seafarers keenly desire to return to our King Hygelac in Geatland. But if I ever hear that the neighbouring tribes mean you harm, I'll bring a thousand thanes to aid you in your hour of need."

Hrothgar answers you then: "Dear Beowulf, you are rich in strength and wise beyond your years, and if spear, sword or sickness should ever take the life of your sovereign lord, your kinsmen, the Storm-folk of Geatland, could not find a better man to be their king and guard their war-hoard than you."

Then Healfdane's son, hoary Hrothgar, Shield of the Spear-Danes, presents you with twelve new treasures from his strong-box. Having embraced the old man, who is like a second father to you now, you take your leave of the King. And despite your protestations, you know, in your heart of hearts, that you will never see each other again.

That ocean-wanderer, your proud ship *Sea-Wolf*, is riding at anchor, waiting for her master, eager to be away over the whale's-way. The wide sea-boat, with soaring prow, is loaded with battle-raiment, warhorses and arms, but the mast still rises high above the gift-hoard.

With every remaining member of your party on board, the *Sea-Wolf* divides the deep water, leaving Denmark behind.

Turn to **383**.

"Dragon!" you say out loud, and immediately feel the blood quicken in your veins.

If you ever find yourself in battle against a dragon or a wyrm, you may add 1 point when calculating your *Combat Rating*.

Gain 1 *Hero Point* and turn to **228**.

Your Geatish storm-warriors bound up the beach, a rope going with them, ring-mail clashing as they drag the *Sea-Wolf* ashore.

Beyond the grey beach rise the black sea-carved cliffs. As you survey the coast a spear-shaft of sunlight breaks through the clouds and you see the flash of armour.

A watchman! Sea guard. Coast warden.

From where he stands on sentry duty, posted there at the regal command of Scyld Scefing's heir, the hawk-sharp watchman witnesses your arrival at the limit of King Hrothgar's domain.

He sees the polished shields of your men as they make their way ashore, and, curious as a cat, he guides his steed down to the shingle. Galloping through the surf, he greets you, holding out his spear at arm's length, and issues his challenge.

"Strangers, you have steered this proud craft through the sea-ways, and come clad as warriors. In all my years as look-out at land's end, I have never known shield-bearers come ashore more brazenly.

"King Hrothgar has had no word of your coming, so tell me your names and your purpose, or you'll go no further!"

How will you react to the Coast Warden's challenge?

If you want to draw your sword, turn to **260**. If you leave your sword sheathed and explain to Hrothgar's look-out the reason for you voyaging to the land of the Danes, turn to **339**.

## 61

You struggle to make yourself heard – over the wind and the rain and the roar of the mountainous sea – and keep the rowers in time, and the wave-cutter's course straight and true.

Roll one die (or pick a card). If the number rolled is odd (or the card is red), turn to **85**. If the number rolled is even (or the card is black), turn to **27**.

## 62

You are not far from the entrance to the cave when your grip on the wave-wracked bluff fails you. You fall from the cliff-face and onto the rough rocks far below.

Your adventure, like your life, is over.

# THE END

## 63

The surviving nicors suddenly break off their attack and the water is filled with squeaking shrieking noises as the hag-fish turn tail and disappear ahead of you along the tunnel. Taking this as a good sign and making the most of the opportunity this provides, you follow, hoping that they might lead you to their dam.

Turn to **81**.

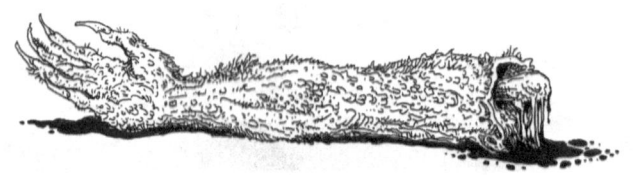

Kicking yourself clear of the monster's jaws, you watch as the hakarl sweeps past below you, its dagger-fin clipping your leg.

As the death-shark comes round again, you tighten your grip on the wound-hoe in your hand and prepare to defend yourself. (In this battle, you have the initiative.)

HAKARL                         COMBAT 7        ENDURANCE 8

You may spend 1 *Hero Point* to ensure that you beat the beast, if you want (turn to **90**), but if not you will have to conduct the fight as normal. If you are victorious, turn to **90**, but if you lose the battle, turn to **15**.


**65**

Lying inside the chest is a rotted leather bag, from which has spilled a mass of gold coins. You do not recognise the kingly image struck into them, and cannot quite decode the runes that ring the regal face.

"Do not touch it, my lord," says Wiglaf the Watchful, peering over your shoulder at the contents of the chest. "We do not want to draw down another curse by stealing from the barrow-king."

If you want to take the gold, regardless of Wiglaf's words of warning, turn to **103**. If you think Wiglaf is probably right, and it is better to leave the treasure lying where it is, turn to **250**.


**66**

The Celtic people of the western isles of Bretland believe that eating the delicate flesh of the salmon imparts knowledge to the one who consumes it.

Write the kenning *Salmon-Wise* on your Adventure Sheet and make a note that if you should ever come across a section number with the symbol of a salmon beneath it, rather than read that section, deduct 50 and turn to this new section instead, before proceeding.

Gain 2 *Endurance* points and then turn to **390**.

### 67

Despite hurling the boulder with all the strength you can muster, your aim is off and it sails past the giant's head.

"Right, that's enough fun and games!" it growls and, hefting its stone club in its misshapen hands, the brute charges towards you at a lumbering run. (In this battle the giant has the initiative.)

ELADA THE ETTIN          COMBAT 6          ENDURANCE 9

If you want to, you may spend 1 *Hero Point* to automatically win your battle against the giant (turn to **49**).

If not, conduct the battle as normal and, if you win, turn to **49**. However, if you lose, turn to **79**.

### 68

You bat the spears aside, as if they were no more bother than marsh-flies, and in more than one case send them flying back at those who are trying to drive you from the hall. And when you are done returning the spears to their masters, you take out your rage on those still standing.

Make a note that you have slain another 6 warriors and then turn to **158**.

### 69

The tunnel straight ahead of you would take you back to the barrow-guard's chamber, so do you want to turn left (turn to **233**), or right (turn to **474**)?

**70**

It feels as if your body is frozen. No matter how hard you strain against whatever magical bonds are holding you, you cannot break free of the sea-hag's spell.

There is nothing you can do as the ogress returns with a large knife and starts to joint you for her cooking pot, while you are still alive.

Your adventure ends, as a meal for Grendel's monstrous mother.

# THE END

**71**

The helmet is ringed about with wire at the crown, creating a rim that will stop the whetstone-sharpened blades of his enemies when a shield-warrior must go into battle against grim foes.

If you find yourself in battle with an enemy using an edged weapon, rather than a mace or their bare hands, you may reduce their *Combat Rating* by 1 point.

Now turn back to **402**.

**72**

You pull yourself through the water as fast as you can, with powerful strokes of your arms and kicking your legs furiously. Seeing a glow permeate the water from above, you surface at last inside another cave. As you do so, your unseen attackers dart back into the darkness of the tunnel.

As you gladly take in great lungfuls of air, you can't help wondering what the creatures are afraid of, because it clearly isn't you.

Turn to **110**.

"Very well," says the King, "I see you have a majestic blade of your own that will doubtless be up to the task. So instead, let me offer you another token, that it might afford you protection."

From the collection of treasures that surrounds his stone bier, the draugr takes an amulet, fashioned in the form of Jormungandr, the world-serpent, holding its tail in its mouth.

"May the greatest of serpents protect you from this hoard-stealing upstart," he says, as he places the talisman over your head.

Add the Serpent Amulet to your Equipment List and make a note that Jormungandr has two eyes fashioned from inset rubies.

Now turn to **105**.

The barrow looms before you, big as a hill, a monument to a king long since dead, his name forgotten. Skirting the perimeter of the mound, you find an entrance to the cairn, a stone archway half hidden where part of the hill has crumbled, and overgrown with long grass.

However, a well-worn goat-track leads from the barrow down towards the edge of the headland where the pagan burial-hall stands. Following the track, you crane you neck to peer over the edge of the cliff and see the entrance to a cave in the sea-washed wall below. It would appear that there is more than one way to enter the Dragon's lair.

Will you return to the entrance to the cairn and gain access to the barrow that way (turn to **114**), or will you risk climbing down the cliff-face to the cave-mouth (turn to **94**)?

You find the perfect hiding place, behind an outcrop of bare rock on the heath, and there you wait for the wyrm.

Hours pass, during which time your muscles become cold and numb out on the desolate heath, unprotected from the chilling wind.

(Lose 1 *Agility* point and 1 *Combat* point.)

But then, eventually, you feel a tremor pass through the ground, followed by another and another, as something large approaches your position.

Turn to **357**.

Cautiously, like a wildcat stalking its prey, you skirt the edge of the cave, your weapon held high, fearing what you might find lying upon the stone.

But rather than headless Aeshere laid there, you see Grendel at rest, lying limp from the fight, his life having wasted away through the wound you dealt him. And laid beside the monster is the arm his mother stole back from King Hrothgar's hall.

You raise the Giant-sword, ready to cleave the fiend's head from his shoulders – to prove to both Danes and Geats that the monster is indeed dead – when the corpse's eyelids flick open and the horror fixes you with the yellow orbs of its eyes.

Turn to **55**.

## 77

You are startled by how quickly the creature can move, considering that it is a corpse! (In this battle, the draugr has the initiative.)

DRAUGR GUARD                  COMBAT 8          ENDURANCE 7

If you wish, you may spend 1 *Hero Point* to automatically win this battle (turn to **99**).

If not, Wiglaf will assist you in your battle against the un-dead guard. Each Combat Round you will have two attacks rather than just one; if one or other of the attacks is successful, you will injure the draugr, but if both attacks are successful, you do double damage that Combat Round. However, the draugr is focusing its attacks against you, so if it wins a Combat Round, you are the one who will be injured and not Wiglaf.

If you defeat your opponent, turn to **99**.


## 78

You watch as the Coast Warden's horse carries him to the top of the cliffs and he rides away to warn King Hrothgar and his karls of your coming. But at least now you know which way to go yourself, and so you set off after the coast guard.

Add the kenning *Wave-Watcher* to your Adventure Sheet and then turn to **273**.


## 79

"Oh!" says Queen Wealhtheow, clearly surprised. "I thought you beat the giants. If you did not, how did you escape their island? Did you run like a cowardly cur? That does not sound like the hero I know. Are you even telling the truth, or is your battle with the giant tribe just some fabrication with which you thought to fool us?"

The Queen does not like being made fun of, and it is your fault that she feels like she has been duped.

Lose 1 *Hero Point*, but restore your *Agility*, *Combat* and *Endurance* scores to what they were before you embarked upon your tale, and then turn to **192**.

## 80

Calling to mind the story of Sigurd and Fáfnir, you recall how there was a weak spot in the wyrm's scale-armour, under its left shoulder.

As the Dragon recoils from your savage strike, you notice a similar point of weakness where the fiendish fire-breather's wing joins its body.

Pushing home your advantage, you rush at the beast and thrust upwards with the broken blade, forcing its jagged point between the Dragon's scales and driving it home with all your berserker-might.

Gain 1 *Hero Point* and turn to **176**.

## 81

You surface again, at long last, inside another cave, and this one is even larger than the last.

Turn to **110**.

You fall asleep and dream of the mighty god of thunder, wielding his hammer Mjolnir against hoary-bearded frost giants and the spawn of Loki, Fenrir the Wolf of Ragnarok and Jormungandr the world-encircling serpent.

Oh to have the strength of Thor!

Record Thor's Favour on your Adventure Sheet, add 2 *Endurance* points, and then turn to **427**.

The warrior's hold on your arm tightens, as he strains with all his might, and you cry out in agony as he starts to break your fingers, one by one.

Lose 2 *Endurance* points and 1 *Combat* point.

*Take a Combat test*, and if you pass the test, turn to **142**, but if you fail the test, turn to **37**.

But one wolf still remains. The creature gives voice to an agonised howl and rises up on its hind-legs, limb-bones reshaping as it does so. Patches of its pelt are absorbed into its body, leaving exposed naked skin, and in some places raw muscles, to your unhappy gaze.

This is no wolf, but a skin-changer. A night-fiend. A man-beast. A Varulfur!

Snarling, the man-beast leaps at you. (In this battle the Varulfur has the initiative.)

VARULFUR     COMBAT 8  ENDURANCE 7

If you want to, you may spend 1 *Hero Point* to automatically win your battle with the inhuman creature (turn to **322**).

If not conduct the battle as normal and, if you win, turn to **54**.

## 85

Thor's hammer pummels the heavens, the storm's wrath worsens, and the *Sea-Wolf* is thrown over the tempest-tossed sea, while lightning, like storm-flash fire, splits the sky.

Until the rumour of land on the horizon becomes the shimmer of sea-beaten cliffs and wave-washed rocks that reach for the *Sea-Wolf* with terrible stone claws.

Turn to **115**.

## 86

There is only one tunnel you haven't yet tried, and so you go that way.

Turn to **474**.

You hurl the rock at the giant.

If you want to ensure that it finds its target, deduct 1 *Hero Point* and turn to **47**.

If not, *Take a Combat test*. If you pass the test, turn to **47**, but if not, turn to **67**.

There are thirty coins altogether.

Make a note of this fact on your Adventure Sheet, and add the Purse of Ancient Coins to your Equipment List, before turning to **250**.

As before, as guests of the hall, you are treated to a glorious feast. (Gain 6 *Endurance* points.)

But while you are enjoying Hrothgar's meat and ale, Unferth approaches, in his cups once again.

"I challenge you, Beowulf!" he roars, and the hall falls silent. "To a battle of riddles!"

Anxious silence is replaced by relieved laughter as the nature of Unferth's challenge is revealed.

If you good-humouredly accept Unferth's challenge, turn to **455**. If you decline, turn to **58**.

Dark blood clouding the water, the hakarl's body sinks back into the depths. As you watch it descend into the night-black abyss, you see other white-fleshed things darting up from the darkness, attracted by the death-scent of the flesh-eater.

The throng of monsters writhes towards you, spiralling through the water in search of flesh. You are going to have to defend yourself once more.

If you want to spend 2 *Hero Points* to escape your dire predicament, and you are able to, turn to **107**. If not, turn to **126**.


## 91

The corselet is a mail-shirt beyond compare, and its polished silver surface will be distracting to anyone who has to face you in battle.

As long as you are wearing the Silver Corselet, if you are injured in battle roll one die (or pick a card). If the number rolled is even (or the card is black), you may reduce the damage done by the injury you have sustained by 1 *Endurance* point.

Return to **402**.


## 92

Taking up the shovel left you by the weapon-smith, under a sky the colour of beaten metal, you start to dig. It is tiring, back-breaking work, even for a warrior as mighty as you.

As you are digging, you see something coming along the road towards you, but it is not the wyrm. It is an old man, with a long white beard and a patch over one eye. You pause in your labour and he asks you what you are doing.

If you want to tell him, turn to **149**. If not, turn to **134**.

A voice from the gate suddenly cries out: "Stop! Cease your fighting!"

All eyes look to the gatehouse, such is the strength and command of the voice, and weapons are lowered when you see an old man standing there, his hair long and his beard white, a circlet of gold about his head. There is no doubt in your mind as to who this man is.

Shield of the Danes. Lord of Heorot. King Hrothgar.

Putting down your sword, you call out to the King: "Brave Hrothgar! I am Beowulf, prince of the Geats, nephew to King Hygelac, your friend and ally in ages past."

There is something like a fire-spark of recognition in the old king's diamond-sharp eyes. "Beowulf? Son of Edgetheow?"

"Even he, my lord."

"Then lay down your arms and be welcome in this place."

Turn to **470**.

Ensuring that your sword and shield are slung securely across your back, you begin your descent, buffeted by the wind and drenched by showers of sea-spray.

*Take an Endurance test.* If you pass the test, turn to **22**. If you fail the test, turn to **62**.

Alternatively, to avoid having to take the test at all, you may spend 1 *Hero Point* and turn to **22** straightaway.

## 95

Your bloodied war-plough comes down on the Dragon's skull with such force that it delivers the worm a baleful blow.

Deduct 4 points from the Dragon's *Endurance* score and then turn to **50**.

## 96

Much as it pains you to do so, you leap over the side and dive into the sea, Naegling still in hand, leaving the *Sea-Wolf* to face her end alone. But that is just one more crime for which you will exact retribution from the dragon!

As the timbers of the ship become charcoal and sink into the sea, and the Dragon returns to its barrow-cave once more, you start to swim for the cliffs atop which the hoard-guardian has its lair, your men unable to catch up with you.

Reaching the rocky shore at last, exhausted though you are, you begin to climb, determined not to let the Dragon get away unpunished.

*Take an Endurance test.* If you pass the test, turn to **22**. If you fail the test, turn to **62**.

Alternatively, to avoid having to take the test at all, you may spend 1 *Hero Point* and turn to **22** automatically.

## 97

As you make a move to search elsewhere, you notice something glinting beside the piece of bark the ogress was using as a chopping board. It is a golden brooch.

If you want to take the Golden Brooch, add it to the Equipment Box on your Adventure Sheet, making a note that it is inset with twelve freshwater pearls.

Hearing a scraping sound – as of talons on stone – you spin around, sword in hand.

Turn to **55**.

## 98

Taking a bow from one of your men, you nock an arrow to the string and pull it taut, the wood creaking as you do so.

If you want to make sure that your arrow finds its mark, deduct 1 *Hero Point* and turn to **151.**

If not, or you do not have any *Hero Points* left to spend, *Take a Combat test*; if you pass the test, turn to **151**, but if you fail the test, your arrow falls short – turn to **78**.

## 99

The draugr having died a second death, you cross the chamber and enter the tunnel on the other side. You follow the new passage as it also bends to the right until you reach a subterranean crossroads.

Do you want to:

| | |
|---|---|
| Turn left? | Turn to **474**. |
| Go straight on? | Turn to **152**. |
| Turn right? | Turn to **233**. |

The dead king's soul-guardians fall, having died a second death, and you start to move towards the door on the far side of the burial chamber. But as you do so, a phantasmal glow, as of marsh-lights, fills the hollow eyes of the King's corpse as he awakens from his death-sleep.

"Who dares wake me from my sleep of years?" the corpse-king challenges you.

Rising from his stone bed, his battle-blade in his hand, the King Under the Hill prepares to show you just how harshly he deals with those who would disturb his slumber of ages.

If you have the kenning *Hard-won-Wisdom* recorded on your Adventure Sheet, turn to **428**.

If not, how do you want to respond? Will you stand up to the Draugr King (turn to **375**), or will you attempt to appease him, in hope of turning his wrath to reason (turn to **396**)?

Sword held high, in single-minded anger you mean to settle with the monster for those stealthy raids it made against Hrothgar's people, the Spear-Danes. (You have the initiative in this battle.)

GRENDEL                      COMBAT 8          ENDURANCE 9

If you wish you may spend 1 *Hero Point* to automatically win your battle with the risen Grendel (turn to **191**). If not, conduct the battle as normal and, if you win, turn to **191**.

## 102

"King Glámr," you say, dropping to one knee and casting your gaze at the ground, "I apologise for disturbing your eternal rest, but I would not have done so were it not a matter of vital import."

Turn to **460**.

## 103

"I warn you, good king, no good will come of this," Wiglaf says as you take the treasure.

There are thirty coins altogether.

Make a note of this fact on your Adventure Sheet and add the Purse of Ancient Coins to your Equipment List. Also record the kenning *Wiglaf's-Warning* on your Adventure Sheet before turning to **250**.

## 104

The wolves lie dead at your feet. Your band has dispatched enough of the prowling predators that the rest of the pack turn tail and flee back into the darkness.

If you have Wulfgar's Curse written on your Adventure Sheet, turn to **84**. If not, roll one die (or pick a card). If the number rolled is odd (or the card is red), turn to **84**. If the number rolled is even (or the card is black), turn to **342**.

It is time to leave the King's burial chamber, for you have a dragon to slay. Through the second door leading from the sepulchre, you find a set of steps cut into the bedrock of the headland and descend them, your torch lighting the way through the water-dripping darkness.

You cannot be far from the dead king's hoard-hall and the serpent-king that has claimed it, and so your mind turns to how best to prepare yourself for the confrontation to come.

Now would be a good time to eat some provisions. You must also decide which sword you want to use to fight the dragon, as you will not be able to change weapons in the heat of battle.

Once you have made your choice and readied yourself, turn to **411**.

**106**

You hurl open the doors of the hall, but are surprised to be greeted by a heavy wooden beam, which swings down from the rafters, suspended on weight-bearing ropes like a battering-ram, with you as its target.

*Take an Agility test.* If you pass the test, you dodge the descending log – turn to **257**. However, if you fail the test, turn to **170**.

Deduct 2 *Hero Points* and then roll one die (or alternatively, pick a card and if it is 7 or above, or a picture card, take it as being worth 6).

If the number generated is 1-5, this is the number of sea-monsters you instantly defeat; turn to **126** to fight the surviving horrors, with those you have already defeated coming from the bottom of the list.

If the number generated is 6, you manage to slay all the flesh-eaters – turn to **154**.

Pointing your sharpened steel at the shortest of the cliff-tall giants, you shout, "I challenge you to a duel! You who set no store by mind-worth, you who defiled the bodies of my men by feasting on their flesh, you who are undeserving of a noble death, nonetheless, I offer you the chance to redeem yourself in single combat!"

A sound like the tumble of shifting stones echoes across the river, and you realise it is the giants' laughter.

The challenged ogre steps forward, hefting its stone club in its misshapen hands, as you assume a fighting stance, your own wound-maker at the ready. (In this battle you have the initiative.)

ELADA THE ETTIN          COMBAT 6          ENDURANCE 9

If you want to, you may spend 1 *Hero Point* to automatically win your battle against the giant (turn to **49**).

If not, conduct the battle as normal and, if you win, turn to **49**. However, if you lose, turn to **79**.

## 109

The Wolfhound is dead, as are the other dogs that had been left to guard the hall. (Add the kenning *Raven-Feeder* to your Adventure Sheet.) But their masters have been alerted to your presence now.

If you have the kenning *Corpse-Maker* written on your Adventure Sheet, turn to **46**. If not, turn to **273**.

## 110

Able to breathe again, you take in your surroundings by the flickering light of a dozen dried moss oyster-shell lamps.

The high-domed chamber is greater even in size than Hrothgar's famous golden-gabled mead-hall. Hanging, curtain-like formations of rock, like the ribs of some great whale, make you feel as if you are inside the belly of the beast.

In front of you, a flat-topped rock breaks the surface of the subterranean lake and beyond that, several strokes away, the floor of the cavern rises above the level of the water.

With your eyes only just above the surface of the water, you scan the far side of the vast cave and see capering shadows cast upon a water-smoothed wall. You can hear slapping footfalls and a cracked voice chanting to itself, although you cannot make out what it is saying.

It can only be Grendel's Mother! You have cornered the mere-wolf in her lair at last!

If you want to take a moment to examine the rocky island in front of you, as stealthily as you can, turn to **136**. If you would rather take the fight to the sea-hag before she even knows you are there, turn to **169**.

## 111

The rune-forged blade is inlaid with gold. During its making it had many charms hammered into it, to ensure that its edge stays sharp and that it always finds its mark.

When you use the Rune-Sword in battle against an enemy, you may add 1 point when calculating your *Combat Rating*.

Now turn back to **402**.


## 112

Sleep comes at last, and you start to dream…

You can see nothing but clouds, or perhaps it is a thick mist, until two ravens come flying towards you from out of the fog. Somehow you know that these carrion-wing messenger-thralls are Huginn and Muninn, servants of the All-Father.

You feel the feather-wind of their wings and the brush of their quills as they pass, and then the clouds drift away and you see yourself in the Hall of the Stag, fighting the monstrous fear-fiend Grendel.

You have eschewed all weapons and are wrestling with the misshapen ogre.

Record Odin's Favour on your Adventure Sheet and then turn to **427**.


## 113

Your name will go down in legend as a brave and noble ruler, but your tale ends here, as the flames claim you and the burning ship becomes your funeral pyre.

Your adventure is over.

# THE END

## 114

Beside the entrance to the dark passage that leads away into the cold earth, half-covered by trailing grasses, is a weather-worn fractured stone.

If you want to take a look at it more closely, turn to **367**. If you just want to get into the barrow and find the Dragon as quickly as possible, before it finds you, turn to **261**.

## 115

Before it can reach the safety of the shingled shore, the *Sea-Wolf* hits the rocks, the jagged black mourn-makers tearing a great hole in the bow of the boat. You are thrown from the deck and onto the rocks yourself, where you slice your arms and legs open on razor-sharp barnacles and knife-like spurs. (Lose 3 *Endurance* points.)

As you stagger, bleeding, onto the shore, to escape the horrors of the sea, you are joined by the rest of your men. However, it soon becomes apparent that one of your fellows did not survive the wrecking.

Deduct 1 from your *Crew* score and then turn to **60**.

Warily you pluck the witch's wooden spoon from the pot and cautiously slurp a mouthful of the mixture.

Having prepared yourself for something vile tasting, you are surprised to discover that it actually tastes quite pleasant – like boiled ham hock and nettles – but this soup is more than just a meal, it is a magical concoction, brewed to increase the strength of anyone who consumes it. (Gain 4 *Endurance* points and 1 *Combat* point.)

However, what you do not realise is that an important ingredient of the potion is the flesh of a mortal warrior – in this case, Aeshere, Hrothgar's counsellor. (Lose 2 *Hero Points*.)

Turn to **97**.

"I slew five giants in total that day, your majesty," you say, finishing your story. (Make a note of this fact on your Adventure Sheet.)

"You are indeed a mighty hero," declares Queen Wealhtheow, smiling sweetly, "and one who has demonstrated that he has brains as well as brawn."

Gain 4 *Hero Points*, restore your *Agility*, *Combat* and *Endurance* scores to what they were before you began your tale, and then turn to **192**.

"I have it!" you declare proudly. "The answer is, an anchor!"

Unferth grunts his displeasure. "Very well, try this one," he says, belching loudly before continuing.

> "Alone I wage war, wounded by steel,
> My master I'll save, though I'll never heal.
> What am I?"

The answer to the riddle is another simple noun. If you know the one-word answer, turn the letters of the word into numbers using the code A=1, B=2… Z=26, add them together, triple the total, and turn to the section with the same number as this final total.

If you cannot fathom the answer, or the section you turn to makes no sense, turn to **392**.

Keeping your arms pinioned to your sides, the ogress carries you to the bottom of the lake. There, with powerful kicks of her webbed feet, she enters a tunnel and you feel that you are being transported upwards again.

And then suddenly there is a flare of light above you and you burst from the chilling depths into a cave, greater even in its dimensions than Hrothgar's golden, gabled hall, and you are able to breathe again.

You are numb from the chilling waters and do nothing to resist the ogress as she drags you from the lake onto the sandy floor of the cave.

The hag leaves you on the silty ground, amidst the remains of dead fish and a half-devoured deer, your cheek pressed against the gritty sand, while she trudges off into a dark corner.

Your body is so numb, you could almost believe that Grendel's mother has cast some pagan spell over you, to keep you from moving…

If you have the kenning *Blood-Curse* recorded on your Adventure Sheet, turn to **70**.

If not, *Take a Hero test*. If you pass the test, turn to **324**. If you fail the test, turn to **70**.

The ogre turns to face his imagined accuser. "Who are you calling weak?" the brute roars.

"I didn't call you weak!" the other bellows back. "Can't you see he's trying to trick you, you idiot?"

"Oh, I'm an idiot now, am I?" the giant says, hefting its great stone club in its hands and charging towards its fellow.

In no time at all, all five giants are fighting among themselves, as the other three pick sides and join the fray.

The jotunn-kin land blow after skull-cracking blow upon each other. And then, when the fight is at its fiercest, the first light of dawn touches the land.

Turn to **137**.

And there, coiled about the treasure-mound, is the worm-serpent you have come here to kill. The smooth scales of its armoured hide gleam gold with the reflected light of the hoard-heap that it clutches to itself like a lover.

It is a terrible creature – all wings, and fangs and tearing talons – but you are King Beowulf – the Bee-Wolf, the Bear, the Berserker – and your vengeful fury will not be denied. Taking up your sword you attack the creature as it lies drowsing, drawing blood before it even knows you are there. (In this battle you have the initiative.)

DRAGON                COMBAT 10      ENDURANCE 48

If you reduce the Dragon's *Endurance* score to 42 points or fewer, or after 4 Combat Rounds (whichever is sooner), turn to **403**.

Alternatively, you may spend 1 *Hero Point* and turn to **403** straightaway.

**122**

The wolf pack lies dead at your feet, your fellow warriors having dispatched the rest of the savage hunters, although one of them has not lived to tell the tale.

(Deduct 1 from your *Crew* score.)

With wounds dressed and blades cleaned, your party is soon on its way again.

The trees eventually start to thin out and then it is not much longer before you emerge on the other side of the forest.

However, before you leave the woods, you manage to forage 2 Meals' worth of provisions, in berries and birds' eggs.

The bleak and boggy moorlands stretch away before you, forming a malodorous quagmire in the shadow of the misty fells. If you are to reach your goal, you have no choice but to set out across them.

Turn to **417**.

## 123

To your left is the passageway that leads back to the barrow-guard's domed chamber. Do you want to follow the tunnel straight ahead of you (turn to **474**), or the one to your right (turn to **152**)?

## 124

The pack comes for you then, out of the night, the eyes of the wolves burning red like the embers of a dying fire, jaws slavering, fiend-called and hunger-savage. You are forced to fend off two of the hunters at the same time. (In this battle, the wolves have the initiative.)

|  | COMBAT | ENDURANCE |
|---|---|---|
| First WOLF | 6 | 7 |
| Second WOLF | 7 | 6 |

You may spend 1 *Hero Point* to win the fight with the Wolves (turn to **104**), otherwise you will have to conduct the battle as normal and only turn to **104** if you win.

## 125

It is time to leave the King's burial chamber, for you have a dragon to slay. Through the second door leading from the sepulchre, you find a set of steps cut into the bedrock of the headland and descend them, your torch lighting the way through the water-dripping darkness.

"We cannot be far from the hoard-hall of that murder-glutton serpent-king," says Wiglaf, his hushed voice still seeming uncomfortably loud as it echoes from the chisel-cut steps.

"Then we must prepare ourselves for the battle to come," you reply.

Now would be a good time to eat some provisions. Wiglaf has a flask of Ypocras, a spiced wine infused with herbs, which acts as a powerful restorative, and which he shares with you.

(Gain 3 *Endurance* points, 1 *Combat* point, 1 *Agility* point, and 1 *Hero Point*.)

You must also decide which sword you want to use to challenge the Dragon, as you will not be able to change weapons during the battle.

Once you have made your choice and readied yourself, turn to **411**.

You must slay the swarming sea-monsters before they kill you. (In this battle you have the initiative, but you must fight the creatures all at the same time.)

|                | COMBAT | ENDURANCE |
|----------------|--------|-----------|
| SEA-SERPENT    | 7      | 7         |
| SCALY-FIEND    | 6      | 6         |
| FANGED-HORROR  | 7      | 5         |
| DEMON-FISH     | 6      | 7         |
| SPINED-BEAST   | 5      | 7         |
| WRITHING-EEL   | 6      | 5         |

If you manage to slay all of these horrific denizens of the deep, turn to **154**. If you lose the battle, turn to **308**.

## 127

*Take a Hero test*. If you pass the test, turn to **95**. If you fail the test, turn to **147**.

## 128

"We killed five giants in total, your majesty," you say, finishing your story. (Make a note of this fact on your Adventure Sheet.)

Hrothgar's Queen looks at you in confusion. "I thought the giant-tribe was brought low by your hand, and yours alone," says Queen Wealhtheow.

Your host is clearly disappointed in you.

Restore your *Agility*, *Combat* and *Endurance* scores to what they were before you began your tale, and then turn to **192**.

### 129

"I am here to return that which was stolen!" you say, holding up the Golden Goblet before the draugr's sightless eye-sockets.

"He who would steal from the lord who lies sleeping here shall suffer his great wrath!" the barrow-guard declares, hefting the ancient weapon in its shrivelled hands.

Turn to **5**.

### 130

Several of the spears bury their sharpened heads in your flesh.

Roll one die and add 1. Deduct this many *Endurance* points. (Alternatively, pick a card and deduct its face value from your *Endurance* score, unless it is 8 or above or a picture card, in which case deduct 7 points from your *Endurance* score.)

Now roll one die again. This is the total number of the spear-throwers you kill. However, if you roll a 6 you have still only slain 5 warriors.

Add the number of Spear-Danes you have killed to the total of number of warriors you have overcome since entering Heorot and turn to **158**.

## 131

The white-maned warhorses are fine battle-steeds indeed, and it goes without saying that when the time is right, you will ride the one bearing the King's jewel-studded war-saddle, the stallion called Alsvior.

Add the kenning *Shadow-Fast* to your Adventure Sheet and turn to **402**.

## 132

Now it is you – Beowulf Beastslayer – whose heart burns with the desire for retribution, and your thirst for vengeance will only be slaked by a dragon's blood!

You order the *Sea-Wolf* – that same proud-rigged, wave-skimmer that carried you across the whale-road to Hrothgar's kingdom all those years ago – to be readied once more. And when all is prepared, your noble storm-warriors board the ship as she strains at her hawsers, hawk-keen to be away once more.

Standing in the bow, with one liver-spotted hand on the carved dragon-head prow, you keep your eyes fixed on the distant headland, where breakers beat against black cliffs, as your men haul on their oars, carrying you over the tumultuous waves towards your destiny.

But even as the *Sea-Wolf* dances over the crashing spume, the Dragon takes to the air a second time, and there is nothing you can do as it bathes that proud wave-dancer with its fiery fury, its terrible flames banishing the arrows the Geats send flying through the tormented air towards it.

The mast and your much-prized bear-banner sail are first to catch light, but soon the boat itself is aflame and the heat licks at your arms and legs.

Will you stand your ground, in the hope that you might lure the dragon closer and encourage it to try to take you from the boat, thereby giving you the opportunity you need to kill it (turn to **113**), or will you abandon ship, along with the rest of the crew (turn to **96**)?

## 133

You lay down and rest your head upon a bolster, as your brave sea-warriors bow to their hall-rest round about you, all apart from Handscio, who remains awake to watch over you all. In no time the silent hall is silent no longer, filled as it is with the snores of you drowsing warriors.

As you wait for sleep to come you consider asking the gods for guidance, but which god? To whom will you pray?

| | |
|---|---|
| Odin the All-Father? | Turn to **112**. |
| Thor, Lord of Thunder? | Turn to **82**. |
| Tyr, God of War? | Turn to **53**. |
| Loki, the Mischief-Maker? | Turn to **401**. |
| Freya, Goddess of Beauty? | Turn to **9**. |
| None of the above? | Turn to **427**. |

## 134

Wishing you well, the old man goes on his way, and you get back to work until, at long last, the pit is dug.

Turn to **226**.

## 135

The contents of the cauldron are bubbling away furiously over the crackling fire raised beneath it. Through the clouds of steamy vapour, the broth appears to be a dark green colour – like boiling swamp water – with globules of fat collecting on the surface. You suspect that it was intended to be the monster's supper.

If you want to taste some of the broth, turn to **116**. If you would rather leave well enough alone, turn to **97**.

## 136

Moving slowly, wary of making even the slightest splash that might alert the ogress to your presence, you reach onto the rock and feel about with your fingers. They close around something hard and smooth, and drawing back your hand you see that you have found a broad-bladed axe.

Add the Axe to the Equipment Box on your Adventure Sheet, making a note that the blade is decorated with the etched heads of four wild boar, and then turn to **169**.

## 137

The instant the sunlight falls upon the giants, an incredible transformation overcomes them. Their skin becomes cold and hard, and grey as granite. Expressions of shock seize their ugly features and then become fixed forever on their faces as their bodies turn to stone.

Leaving the giant-tribe mineralised where they stand, now looking like nothing more than a cluster of standing-stones, you and your men return to the shore, and find the *Sea-Wolf* straining at its moorings, eager to be away across the whale-road once more…

Turn to **117**.

## 138

You find Hrothgar's company sleeping after their feast, but at your startling arrival, they rouse themselves in an effort to escape your wrath.

Roll one die. This is the number of men you manage to kill as your enter Heorot. However, if you roll a 6 you have still only killed 5 warriors.

Make a note of how many men you have killed and then turn to **347.**

With you trapped in her cruel clutches, this mere-wolf drags you down even deeper into the freezing depths of the lake.

If you have Njord's Favour recorded on your Adventure Sheet, or you are wearing a Fish Talisman, turn to **119**.

If not, *Take an Endurance test*; if you pass the test, turn to **119**, but if you fail the test, turn to **13**.

### 140

The *Sea-Wolf* leaps over the waves before the sea-beast, as it continues to plough through the storm-tossed spume on its way to King Hrothgar's kingdom. But to tell your men to run from the monster is not in the brave and noble manner of the hero you purport to be. (Lose 1 *Hero Point*.)

Besides, even a ship as swift as yours cannot outrun the hunting whale. The Orca dives below the waves again only to ram the ship from below, setting your men swearing "By Odin's beard!" and "Thor's hammer!"

Through the lashing rain, beyond the unsettled sea, you can see a shadow on the skyline.

Do you want to command your men to keep rowing, and hope you reach land before the whale can capsize the boat (turn to **177**), or will you now prepare to meet the Orca's attack with your sword (make a note that the Orca has the initiative and turn to **217**)?

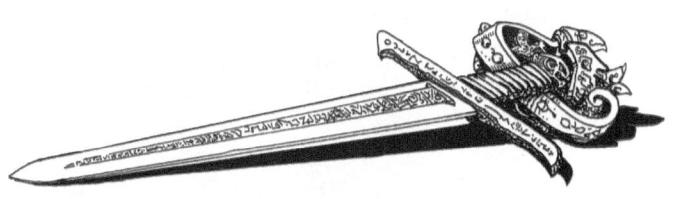

And there, coiled about the treasure-mound, is the worm-serpent you have come here to kill. The smooth scales of its armoured hide gleam gold with the reflected light of the hoard-heap that it clutches to itself like a lover.

It is a terrible creature – all wings, and fangs and tearing talons – but you are King Beowulf – the Bee-Wolf, the Bear, the Berserker – and your vengeful fury will not be denied. Taking up your sword you attack the creature as it lies drowsing, drawing blood before it even knows you are there. (In this battle you have the initiative.)

DRAGON                          COMBAT 10      ENDURANCE 48

Wiglaf will aid you in battling the Dragon. Each Combat Round you will have two attacks rather than just one; if you win either you will injure the Dragon, but if you win both, you do double damage for that Combat Round. However, the Dragon is focusing its attacks against you, so if it wins a Combat Round, you will be the one who comes to harm.

If you reduce the Dragon's *Endurance* score to 42 points or fewer, or after 4 Combat Rounds (whichever is sooner), turn to **403**.

Alternatively, you may spend 1 *Hero Point* and turn to **403** straightaway.

Driven into a frenzy by the pain of Beowulf's twisting hold on your arm, you claw at the unarmoured hero with your free hand. Raking his flesh with your rough claws, forcing him to loosen his grip on your scaly limb, you break free at last.

If you have the kenning *Geat-Guard* written on your Adventure Sheet, turn to **368**. If not, turn to **182**.

Every muscle in your body tensing, with a raw bellow, you raise the boulder from the ground and then prepare to throw it.

But will you hurl it across the river (turn to **155**), or directly at your opponent (turn to **87**)?

The howling of the monster echoes from the black shapes of the high fells, and is answered by a chorus of wolves from somewhere nearby.

If you have Wealhtheow's Blessing or Odin's Favour recorded on your Adventure Sheet, turn to **342**, unless you have Wulfgar's Curse recorded as well, in which case turn to **124**.

If you have none of these things written on your Adventure Sheet, turn to **124** anyway.

"Heremod's rule brought not pleasure but a plague upon our people," Hrothgar begins, "and death and destruction to the Danish tribes. In his fits he would cut down his comrade in war and his table-companion alike, until that famous prince turned away from the feastings of men.

"Inwardly, his heart-hoard grew raw and blood-thirsty – no rings did he give to the Danes for his mind's-worth – and he lived as an outcast, paying the penalty for his persecution of his people by having to endure a life of sorrow.

"Learn from this, beloved Beowulf! Practise generosity! Put away arrogance, for the noon of your strength shall last for now, but in a little time sickness or a sword will strip it from you all too soon.

"So it is with myself. I shepherded the Ring-Danes for fifty years, defending them in war – with ash and with edge, over the earth's breadth – against many nations, until I numbered at last not a single adversary beneath the skies' expanse. But what change of fortune befell me at my hearth with the coming of Grendel. Grief sprang from joy when the fell-hearted foe entered our golden hall of Heorot! Great was the pain that persecution thrust upon me."

Record the kenning *Hard-won-Wisdom* on your Adventure Sheet.

"But come now," says the King, "take your place at the bench."

If you now want to ask to hear tales of Sigmund's great deeds, turn to **165**. If you would prefer to take your seat, as the King has bidden you, turn to **89**.

### 146

A man, dressed in the fine garb of one of the King's thanes stands watch over the gates of Heorot, alongside the guards on sentry duty there.

"My lord!" the Coast Warden calls from the front of your party. "I bring travellers from beyond the sea, who seek audience with King Hrothgar."

He turns to you then and says, "Here I must leave you, for I must return to the cliffs to watch for sea-raiders. May the gods smile on you in your great undertaking and Njord bring you safely back to your brave ship once more."

With that he turns his horse about and departs.

(Record Njord's Favour on your Adventure Sheet.)

"I am Wulfgar, Hrothgar's herald," calls the karl from atop the gatehouse. "Who shall I say seeks audience with the King?"

You step up to the gate, spear in hand, and your shield on your arm.

"I am Beowulf, prince of the Geats, kin of King Hygelac, and if you will permit us an audience with your gracious King Hrothgar, we will explain in full the reason why we have braved the storm-tossed seas to journey to the land of the Danes."

Turn to **363**.


## 147

Your bloodied war-plough comes down on the Dragon's skull with such force that the blade, ancient and silver-streaked, bursts asunder.

Make a note that from now on you must deduct 1 point when calculating your *Combat Rating*.

If you have the kenning *Wyrm's-Weakness* recorded on your Adventure Sheet, turn to **80**. If not, turn to **50**.


## 148

Your battle with the giants is worthy of the sagas of your people, and finally the last of them lies dead beside the river.

You return to the shore, where the *Sea-Wolf* is already a-sea, straining at the leash of its chain to be away across the whale-road once more…

Turn to **128**.


## 149

You see no harm in telling the old man of your plan to kill the wyrm, and after a moment's pondering, looking at the pit, in a voice cracked with age he says, "Rather than just one pit, you should try digging a series of ditches. That way, the wyrm's blood will be able to flow away freely and not drown you in your pit."

If you want to follow the old man's advice, turn to **162**. If you would rather stick to Reginn's original plan, turn to **134**.

## 150

The dead king's soul-guardians fall, having died a second death, and you start to move towards the door on the far side of the burial chamber. But as you do so, a phantasmal glow, as of marsh-lights, fills the hollow eyes of the King's corpse as he awakens from his death-sleep and challenges you.

"Hwā dearr mē weccan fram gēara slǣpe?"

Gif þū canst understandan hwæt se cyning segþ, wend tō ān hund.

Rising from his stone bed, his battle-blade in his hand, the King Under the Hill prepares to show you just how terrible his great wrath can be.

Turn to **178**.

## 151

Your arrow flies straight and true, hitting the fleeing Coast Warden in the back of his neck and sending him toppling from his horse. He won't be warning anyone about your arrival.

Ordering your men to bring their long ashen spears and war-shields with them, you follow the path to the top of the black cliffs and from there set off in search of King Hrothgar's fabled mead-hall.

But do you want to approach proudly, unafraid of who might see you (turn to **232**), or do you want to wait until dusk and then creep up to Hrothgar's house, like a band of thieves in the night (turn to **6**)?

## 152

Proceeding along the new passageway, you find that it too begins to bend to the right and, continuing to follow it, you soon find yourself standing before a great rift in the ground. You can only imagine in ages past subsidence disturbed the resting place of the King interred beneath the hill. (Record the kenning *Earth-Maw* on your Adventure Sheet.)

If you are going to proceed any further along the tunnel, you are going to have to leap the chasm. But it will be no easy matter – the crevasse must be at least the height of two men across.

If you want to attempt to jump across the chasm, turn to **256**. If you think it wiser to return to the tunnel crossing and choose another way to go, turn to **328**.

Your sword-blade suddenly starts to glow, as if imbued with the power of the storm, the blazing white light picking out the runes and other decorations etched into the iron.

With the weapon held out before you like a torch, you make your way towards the clearly illuminated entrance to the underwater tunnel.

Entering the tunnel, you are surprised to see the scintillating light from your sword reflected from the bulbous white eyes of a shoal of hideous fish-things. They have distended jaws and spiny fish-like tails, but in place of fins they have spindly arms that end in raking talons. Each is no bigger than a pike, but there are a lot of them.

If you have Njord's Favour recorded on your Adventure Sheet, or you are wearing a Fish Talisman, turn to **16**. If not, turn to **44**.

Those scaly flesh-eaters will not dine upon Beowulf this day! Daylight will find their bifurcated bodies cast up amidst the driftwood on beaches up and down the coast.

Surfacing again, you find Sol's beacon brightening the sky to the east. The billows sink, revealing the windy cliffs of the headland. But there is no sign of Breca, your rival having left you far behind. There is no hope of catching up with him now.

Exhausted by your battle with the sea-monsters, you let the tide carry you away on its currents…

\*   \*   \*   \*

"So you lost the race," says Unferth.

"I slew seven sea-monsters," you tell him. (Make a note of this fact on your Adventure Sheet.) "Not even a whisper has reached me that you have ever survived such a perilous encounter, or of any such deed of daring accomplished in your name. You have only wetted your blade with the blood of your own, Unferth Kinslayer!"

Your Geatish warriors burst into laughter on hearing your taunt, while Unferth's allies remain silent and sullen.

Gain 2 *Hero Points*, restore your *Agility*, *Combat* and *Endurance* scores to what they were before you embarked upon your tale, and then turn to **345**.

## 155

The boulder lands with a thud on the other side of the river.

"My go," grunts the giant.

Your opponent picks up a boulder four times as large as the one you were trying to shift, with one huge hand, and with a grunt of effort hurls it far out of sight.

"You lose!" the brute roars.

"How do you know?" you challenge the giant.

Your opponent looks at you, its lumpen brows knitting in confusion. "What d'you mean?"

"I didn't see where it landed, so how do I know you actually beat me?"

"It went miles," protests the giant.

"Well if that's true, show me where it landed and, if you did indeed throw your rock further than mine, then I will be happy to agree that you have won our weightlifting contest."

"Come on then," says the giant, lumbering off across the river. "Follow me!"

You set off after the giant, you and your men running to keep up with it. The rest of the giant-tribe follow too.

You pass the spot where your boulder ended up and keep running, across the moor.

"There!" says the giant, stumbling to a halt, and putting its huge hands on its huge knees as it pants for breath. It points. "There it is."

And as you lay eyes on the huge rock, half sunk in the peaty turf, the first golden rays of the rising sun touch the island.

Turn to **137**.

## 156

You enter the lightless chapel alone and, lighting a tallow candle there, kneel before the icon of the Lord, nailed to a tree. You beseech the Lord to help you defeat this Devil, which has taken the form of a dragon, in this, your greatest hour of need.

But has He heard your heartfelt-prayers? Only time will tell.

Record The Lord's Favour on your Adventure Sheet but cross off any other Favours you may have recorded there; the Lord God is the only god and you shall have no other gods before Him.

Now turn to **14**.

## 157

Hunger has made the wolves savage and bold. You find yourself forced to fight two of the hunters at the same time. (In this battle, the wolves have the initiative.)

|              | COMBAT | ENDURANCE |
|--------------|--------|-----------|
| First WOLF   | 6      | 7         |
| Second WOLF  | 7      | 6         |

You may spend 1 *Hero Point* to win the fight with the wolves (turn to **122**), otherwise you will have to conduct the battle as normal and only turn to **122** if you actually win.

What remains of Hrothgar's company faces you now, warriors clad in their ring-mail, with weapons in hand, ready to cut you down where you stand and hang your entrails from the rafters.

Deduct the total number of men you have already dealt with from 30, and whatever is left is the total number of warriors you will have to face in battle.

If you have the kenning *Life-Harm* recorded on your Adventure Sheet, turn to **238**. If not, you must now fight King Hrothgar's thanes, and in this battle you have the initiative.

WARRIORS    COMBAT (special)   ENDURANCE (special)

The Warriors' combined *Endurance* score is equal to the number of Hrothgar's men that are still standing after your assault on the King's hall. Their combined *Combat* score has a base level of 6, but for every five Warriors still in the fight, that score is increased by 1 point.

So, for example, if there are seventeen Warriors still standing, they will have a combined *Combat* score of 9 and a combined *Endurance* score of 17. If there are twenty-four Warriors still standing, they will have a combined *Combat* score of 10 and a combined *Endurance* score of 24. But if there are only seven Warriors still standing, they will have a combined *Combat* score of 7 and a combined *Endurance* score of 7.

If you defeat the Spear-Danes, turn to **199**.

## 159

The monster is truly terrible to behold. It enters the hall, ducking its misshapen head to pass below the lintel, and when it stands upright again, its scaly scalp scrapes the rafters.

The monster comes, its hulking form long-limbed, sinew-knotted, and corded all about with muscle. With wyrm-scales, bear-claws, and a beast's hide it comes. And in its eyes burns the fire of hatred of all things merry and mirthful.

*Take a Hero test*. If you pass the test, turn to **209**. If you fail the test, turn to **189**.

## 160

As the hakarl drags you into the lightless depths, you fight to free yourself from its bone-crushing jaws.

If you want to spend 1 *Hero Point* to escape your fate, deduct it from your total and turn to **39**.

If not, *Take a Combat test*, and if you pass the test, turn to **39**. However, if you fail the test, turn to **18**.

## 161

The Golden Torc is a beautiful piece of jewellery, the two ends of the twisted metal strands fashioned into the heads of snarling wolves.

Record the kenning *True-Sight* on your Adventure Sheet and then return to **402**.

## 162

Seeing the wisdom of the old man's advice, you set about digging more holes in the ground. The sweat beading on your brow, you take a break to thank the old man, only to discover that he has vanished.

(Write the kenning *Ditch-Digger* on your Adventure Sheet.)

Resuming your work, you hope that you can finish the series of ditches before the wyrm comes this way, heading to the glassy-pool to drink.

*Take an Endurance test.* If you pass the test, turn to **226**. If you fail the test, turn to **204**.

Alternatively, to avoid having to take the test at all, you may spend 1 *Hero Point* and turn to **226** straightaway.


## 163

"I am here to kill the dragon!" you declare.

"That may be so," counters the barrow-guard, "but first you will have to test your mettle against Grettir of the Draugr!"

Turn to **5**.


## 164

And now there is nothing to do but wait for the mirth-hater to arrive. How will you while away the time while you wait?

| | |
|---|---|
| Try to sleep? | Turn to **133**. |
| Command your men to sing songs to raise their spirits? | Turn to **462**. |
| Simply sit and wait in silence? | Turn to **447**. |

"Very well," says the King, "but take your place at the feast and I will command the skald to sing the Lay of Sigmund."

You and your warriors join the Danes at the feast while the poet takes up his harp and recites the legend of Sigmund. But as the telling continues, the wondrous exploits of the father are soon exceeded by those of his son, Sigurd the Wyrmslayer, and last of the Völsungs.

"You remember how the dvergr Reginn wanted revenge against the wyrm Fáfnir, who had murdered his father and stolen his family's gold, that was a gift from the gods?" sings the skald. "And you remember how the young warrior Sigurd, of the Völsung clan, promised he would slay the wyrm, if the dwarf would forge a sword for him that was worthy of the task? And you remember how Sigurd took the pieces of his father's broken sword – shattered by Odin the All-Father himself – and gave them to Reginn, who forged from them a new sword, Gram – which means 'Wrath' in the old tongue – that cut through the weapon-smith's anvil? Then let me tell you how Sigurd best Fáfnir the wyrm in battle…"

Make a note of your current *Agility*, *Combat* and *Endurance* scores and then turn to **11**.

You cry out in pain as the sea-hag's splintered fingernails sink into your arms and chest, your scream escaping as precious bubbles of air that race for the surface far above.

Lose 4 *Endurance* points and, if you are still alive, turn to **139**.

It is no good, you cannot work out the answer to the riddle. And no matter how hard you beat your fists against the door, the stone will not relent and open for you. (Lose 1 *Hero Point*.)

But having come so far, you are not going to give up now. You are the Shepherd of the Storm-folk. You are the King of Geatland. You are Beowulf Beastslayer, and you will find another way to penetrate the Ravager's lair.

Making your way back through the barrow, you emerge once more on the wind-swept headland. Finding the snow-dusted goat-track again, you follow it to the edge of the rugged bluffs. The cave-mouth lies below your current position, and it is by this ingress that you will enter the Dragon's hoard-hall.

Turn to **94**.

You and your men bring steel blades and iron-headed axes to bear against the jotunn-kin, presenting ring-mail and boar-helms to the blunt blows of the ogres' crude weapons.

First one falls, and then another, but as the remainder of your party take on a pair of the foul fiends, you find yourself facing the biggest and ugliest of the giants, the chieftain of the tribe. (The ogre has the initiative in this battle.)

GIANT CHIEFTAIN             COMBAT 9       ENDURANCE 12

If you manage to slay the giant, turn to **148**.

You haul yourself out of the lake onto the silty floor of the cave, sword in hand. There is a sudden commotion of sound, like webbed feet scampering over stones, and then an abrupt silence.

Realising how exposed your position is, you warily peer around the cave. At the far end, within a space that is almost a secondary chamber off the main one, you catch the glint and glimmer of gold – no doubt treasure offered at the lake to appease the spirits that haunt its depths, and collected magpie-like by the ogress who has dwelt here for who knows how many ages.

To your left you can see a large iron pot hanging over a crackling fire; it is this that cast the capering shadows on the wall – only there are no capering shadows anymore. To your right you can make out a body lying on a rocky ledge, but before you can investigate, to see whether it is all that remains of Hrothgar's trusted counsellor Aeshere, your attention is drawn by something moving on the other side of the cave.

You stare, in disbelief, as your eyes alight upon a slender figure approaching you from the flickering darkness. The figure is that of a young woman, lithe, firm of flesh, with a cascade of golden hair tumbling down about her shoulders, and she is clothed only in shadows.

"What is this?" she says in a voice that is all milk and honey. "A brave warrior come seeking me in my lair at the bottom of the lake of woe?" The air about you is suddenly heady with the sweet scent of honeysuckle.

If you have the kenning *True-Sight* or Freya's Favour recorded on your Adventure Sheet, turn to **219**. If not, turn to **196**.


### 170

The blunt end of the roughly-finished beam hits you in the middle of the chest, sending you flying back out of the hall.

Roll one die and add 1. Deduct this many *Endurance* points. (Alternatively, pick a card and deduct its face value from your *Endurance* score, unless it is 8 or above or a picture card, in which case deduct 7 points from your *Endurance* score.)

If you are still alive, turn to **257**.

"The answer is a shield!" you announce with unabashed delight.

Turn to **252**.

Proceeding along the new passageway, you find that it too begins to bend to the right and, continuing to follow it, you soon find yourself standing before a great rift in the ground. You can only imagine in ages past subsidence disturbed the resting place of the King interred beneath the hill. (Record the kenning *Earth-Maw* on your Adventure Sheet.)

If you are going to proceed any further along the tunnel, you are going to have to leap the chasm. But it will be no easy matter – the crevasse must be at least as far across as the height of two men.

"I say we should turn back," says Wiglaf the Wary. "I have a feeling, deep in my bones, that we are going the wrong way."

If you want to try to jump across the chasm anyway, turn to **205**. If you think it wiser to return to the crossing of the ways and choose another route to take, turn to **328**.

Bringing the blade down in a furious executioner's arc, you take the ogress fully across the neck, breaking the bones therein, as the steel shears through the monster's death-doomed flesh. She falls to the ground, the Giant-sword gory with her blood.

The hag's head rolls across the ground, stopping at your feet. The ogress's eyes look up into yours, and, along with a bloody gruel, the thin hiss of a curse escapes her spluttering lips.

> "Fȳres and flōdes fēounge þola,
> mid þīnum blōde brimrād rēadie!"

With her final breath Grendel's Mother has cursed you. (Record the Sea-hag's Curse on your Adventure Sheet.)

At the same time, the lamps positioned around the cave flame brighter, and the chamber is illumined with a clearness such as the candle of heaven sheds in the sky. By the flaring light, you begin to scour the sea-hag's dwelling.

Do you want to examine the cooking pot (turn to **135**), or do you want to take a closer look at the body you can see lying on a plinth-like ledge against the right-hand wall of the cave (turn to **76**)?

### 174

Offering the gods your great strength, swearing to rid the world of monsters, you beseech the gods to help you in your hunt and one of them answers.

(Record Odin's Favour on your Adventure Sheet.)

Rising from your knees before the shrine, you remount your horse and set off again after the fleeing monster.

Roll one die (or pick a card). If the number rolled is odd (or the card is red), turn to **144**. If the number rolled is even (or the card is black), turn to **342**.

### 175

Now it is you – Beowulf Beastslayer – whose heart burns with the desire for revenge.

You and your men ride northwards, towards the dominion of the Dragon, the desolation birthed by its burning breath. And there upon the snow-clad moors you come upon a shrine to the newest god to claim possession of the souls of the people of this land – the Roman god, known to those who venerate

Him as the Lord – the cross atop the chapel's wooden roof free of snow.

The servants of the Lord believe the dragon to be an incarnation of the Devil, a demon that now lays claim to Hel's dominions.

If you want to stop and pray at the shrine, turn to **156**. If you would prefer to keep riding for the dragon's lair, turn to **14**.

### 176

The beast is beaten back by your berserker blows, until it rallies, determined to meet its end fighting, sensing that its life-force is almost spent.

As you prepare to deliver the fatal stroke, the Dragon's head darts forward on its long neck. The sly serpent catches you in its mouth and bites down hard.

Your armour protects you from the worst of what injuries you might have sustained, but one of the Dragon's fore-fangs pierces your neck, injecting its fiery venom. Gore gushes in waves, and you are drenched in your own life's-blood.

If you are wearing a Serpent Amulet, you will have a number associated with that particular artefact; turn to the section with the same number now.

If you are not wearing a Serpent Amulet, turn to **380**.

### 177

Despite your men rowing with all their might, the *Sea-Wolf* cannot outrun the whale. As you come within sight of the shore, the Orca rams the boat again, driving it towards the jagged rocks that wait to bite down upon its unguarded planks with terrible teeth of stone.

Turn to **115**.

This king, strong in ages past, and strong in spirit now, throws himself at you with the nimbleness of a cat. You would not have expected such a thing possible of one of the un-dead.

He raises his kingly sword in semi-skeletal hands and you see runes etched into its surface blaze with the same witch-light that fills the draugr's eye-sockets. Giving voice to a booming war-cry, he commences his attack. (In this battle, the Draugr King has the initiative.)

DRAUGR KING            COMBAT 9       ENDURANCE 9

If you have Tyr's Favour, you may add 1 point when calculating your *Combat Rating*, for the duration of this battle.

If you wish, you may spend 1 *Hero Point* to automatically win this battle (turn to **416**).

If not, conduct the battle as normal and only if you win, turn to **416**.

Savaged to death by the sea-hag's fish-spawn offspring, the horrors make short work of stripping the flesh from your bones, leaving your sword and armour to sink to the floor of the flooded tunnel, never to be reclaimed.

Your adventure is over.

# THE END

## 180

"I am Beowulf, King of the Geats!" you declare.

"I recognise no such upstart usurper!" the barrow-guard counters. "Glámr is King Under the Hill!"

Turn to **5**.

## 181

The standard is an exquisite piece of work and has the image of a great bear embroidered upon it. Any who see such a banner carried into battle among their company cannot help but be inspired to mighty feats and heroic deeds by the flapping standard.

Write the kenning *War-Rage* on your Adventure Sheet and then turn back to **402**.

## 182

Suddenly the sleeping sentry from the entrance to the hall is there behind you, spear in hand, thrusting the point of it into your unnatural flesh. (Lose 4 *Endurance points.*)

If you are still alive, you bat the weak warrior away and fix your blazing yellow gaze on the young champion and would-be beast-slayer. You have a new blood-feud to occupy you now. (In this battle, Beowulf has the initiative.)

BEOWULF                          COMBAT 10          ENDURANCE 10

If you win the battle with the warrior-hero, turn to **450**.

## 183

Despite the ogress fastening her hooks into you, no harm comes to your hale body – the silver harness rings you round about so tightly that she cannot drive her dire fingers through it.

However, just because your physical form is so protected, that does not mean you cannot drown.

Turn to **139**.

## 184

As you lift the lid of the chest, a spring-loaded mechanism fires a dart, but the tiny projectile flies past you, as you twist out of the way just in time.

Turn to **45**.

## 185

Which sword are you using to fight the Dragon?

| | |
|---|---|
| Angurvadal? | Turn to **147**. |
| Naegling? | Turn to **127**. |
| Neither of these? | Turn to **95**. |

## 186

Taking off your belt, you lay your sword at the foot of King Hrothgar's vacant throne, and swear that you will not pick it up again until the demon is dead.

"What are you doing, my lord?" asks one of your men, Handscio.

"To shorten Grendel's life with a slashing blade would be too simple a business," you tell him. "The monster knows nothing of iron-forged weapons, or the shattering of a shield-wall. If he dares challenge me without a weapon, then I shall face him in the same fashion."

Gain 1 *Hero Point* and make a note that you are no longer carrying your sword, before turning to **164**.

## 187

Your men are spurred on to perform great deeds of heroism, determined not to let anything stop you from fulfilling your oath to the King.

Turn to **122**.

## 188

With a cry of "Forward men, and honour the fallen with the slaughter of their murderers!" you lead the charge against the giants.

If you are both willing and able, you may spend 2 *Hero Points* to swing the battle in your favour (turn to **148**). If not, turn to **168**.

## 189

The sudden violent arrival of the monster and its appearance, hideous in its frightfulness, even makes an experienced monster-hunter such as you doubt the sense in bringing your men to this cursed hall.

Your faith in your own ability to defeat this guzzler of gizzards and grinder of gristle has been shaken to the very marrow in your bones.

Lose 1 *Combat* point and 1 *Hero Point*, and turn to **209**.

## 190

The hakarl drags your lifeless body back into the depths, where it will devour your corpse, undisturbed by the other flesh-eaters of the deep…

Turn to **308**.

The monster's corpse gapes open as it suffers the death-stroke from the hard-swung sword, and with your final blow you separate the head from the body.

Blood, as thick and black as tar, spurts from Grendel's severed neck. Where it has touched the blade of the ancient Giant-sword, the blood hisses, melting the steel with its acid touch, until the sword has dwindled into deadly icicles and the war-tool has wasted away, all except for its hilt.

Now you understand the hag's purpose in recovering her son's arm. She was intending to raise Grendel to life again! But thanks to you the monster is dead once more, as is its mother.

Taking the monster's head up by the hair, you take your prize and prepare to leave the lake-hag's lair. But you cannot ignore the fact that there are all manner of wonderful treasures heaped all around.

You will not be able to carry much, but if you want to take something from the ogress's treasure-hoard, turn to **211**. If not, turn to **231**.

## 192

With the feast at its height, the Queen offers you the ceremonial drinking-cup once again, inviting you, in friendly fashion, to drink.

"We have drunk your health, my lord," she says. "Now drink, and know that you will forever be welcome within the golden hall of Heorot."

Will you accept the cup and drink (turn to **242**), or politely decline the Queen's offer of wine (turn to **274**?

## 193

And there, coiled about the treasure-mound, is the worm-serpent you have come here to kill. The smooth scales of its armoured hide gleam gold with the reflected light of the hoard-heap that it clutches to itself like a lover.

Hearing the jingling of your war-harness, and the tramp of your footsteps on the floor of the earthen hall, the Dragon stirs and opens one eye.

In an instant it turns its monstrous head towards you and, opening its jaws, the breath of the Dragon issues from its throat in a fiery gust.

Are you carrying the Dragon Shield? If so, turn to **295**. If not, turn to **327**.

Ensuring you have your sword with you, you rush out into the night, followed by half a dozen of your men. By the light of the full moon that hangs overhead, you see the blood-trail left by the fleeing fen-lurker glistening like oil upon the ground, and the deep indentations of the ogre's footprints.

You have no intention of letting the murderous visitor get away! And so you mount the horses that the Danes hurriedly bring you from the stables, and set off after the wounded night-stalker.

Despite being mortally wounded, the monster moves as fast as a wolf and is able to keep ahead of you. The only signs you have that you are still in pursuit are the blood-splattered trail it leaves behind it and the plaintive howls of the monster that cut through the waning night.

You have soon left Heorot far behind and pass from the cultivated fields of Hrothgar's people to the untamed moorlands where the wild things are. But before the beaten track peters out entirely, you come upon a wayside shrine.

If you want to stop and make an offering to the gods, turn to **174**. If you would rather maintain your pursuit of the cursed one, turn to **144**.

A man, dressed in the fine clothes and furs of one of the King's thanes, stands at the gates to the palisade wherein lies Heorot.

"I am Wulfgar, herald to King Hrothgar," the nobleman calls from atop the gatehouse. "What is your business here? You come clad in coats of chainmail and masked war-helms, bearing embellished shields, but do you come as friends or foes?"

You step up to the gate, spear in hand, and your shield on your arm.

"I am Beowulf, prince of the Geats, kin of King Hygelac of the Storm-folk, and if you will allow us an audience with the gracious King Hrothgar, we will explain why we have braved the storm-tossed seas to journey to the land of the Danes."

Turn to **363**.

## 196

"Put down your sword," the elfin-beauty tells you, "you have no need of that here. I will not harm you."

If you have the kenning *Blood-Curse* recorded on your Adventure Sheet, turn to **236**.

If not, *Take a Hero test*. If you pass the test, turn to **219**, but if you fail the test, turn to **236**.

## 197

Your furious attack is enough to discourage the water-snakes from attacking you again, and those slithering serpents that you have not yet sliced into bloody chunks retreat to the dark depths once more.

You have no idea how far down the lake-bottom lies – no man does! – but you swim on. As you peer into the depths, you make out the shadow of something moving towards you at an astonishing speed.

That grim and greedy guardian of the flood, keeping her hungry hundred-season watch, has sensed your presence within the water, and before you can do anything to defend yourself she grabs you.

If you are wearing the Silver Corselet, turn to **183**, but if not, turn to **166**.

This king, strong in ages past, and strong in spirit now, throws himself at you with the nimbleness of a cat. You would not have expected such a thing possible of one of the un-dead.

He raises his kingly sword in semi-skeletal hands and you see runes etched into its surface blaze with the same witch-light that fills the draugr's eye-sockets. Giving voice to a booming war-cry, he commences his attack. (In this battle, the Draugr King has the initiative.)

DRAUGR KING                    COMBAT 9          ENDURANCE 9

If you have Tyr's Favour, you may add 1 point when calculating your *Combat Rating*, for the duration of his battle.

If you wish, you may spend 1 *Hero Point* to automatically win this battle (turn to **416**).

If not, Wiglaf will assist you in your battle against the King Under the Hill. Each Combat Round you will have two attacks rather than just one; if one or other of the attacks is successful, you will injure the draugr, but if both attacks are successful, you do double damage in that Combat Round. However, the draugr is focusing its attacks against you, so if it wins a Combat Round, you are the one who will suffer the edge of its blade.

If you defeat your opponent, turn to **416**.

Hrothgar's men lie dead at your feet, ravaged by terrible wounds, and the floor runs red with rivers of wolf-wine.

And then you are away from that accursed hall, fast as the wolf, carrying homeward your glut of slaughter. Seeking out your own cavern-hall, you feast on the bodies of the men you have slain.

Roll one die, or pick a card (and if it is greater than 6 or a picture card, then 6 is the number you have picked), add 6 to the number and gain this many *Endurance points*.

Now roll one die again (or pick a card), and if the number rolled is odd (or the card is red), turn to **215**, but if the number rolled is even (or the card is black), turn to **379**.

**200**

Taking the left branch, you follow the tunnel as it curves to the right and you enter a circular chamber walled with stone. On the opposite side of the chamber another tunnel leads away deeper into the barrow complex, but before you can reach that you will have to get past the guard who must have stood here, on sentry duty, through three hundred winters or more.

It looks like a warrior – clad in rusted ring-mail and with a corroded blade of ancient iron gripped tight in one hand – but it is also quite clearly a corpse. Its body is dust-dry, rid of all moisture, its muscles and sinews exposed as knotted tree-roots that wind about its limbs, while its eye-sockets are empty.

And then it speaks in a cracked voice: "Who would defile the tomb of the mighty Troll-slayer, the famous Taker of Heads?"

How will you answer the barrow-guard's challenge?

| | |
|---|---|
| "I am Beowulf, King of the Geats!" | Turn to **180**. |
| "I am here to kill the dragon!" | Turn to **163**. |
| "I am here to return that which was stolen!" | Turn to **129**. |

**201**

With you having been honoured, Heorot is set out for a hero's banquet. And what a banquet it is! Happiness fills the hall again, while bench-mirth rings to the rafters and the bearers pour wonderful wine from skill-wrought vessels.

Hrothgar rewards not only you, but also the men of your battle-company, granting to each a valuable ancient heirloom and ordering the keeper of his coffers to pay blood-gilt for those cruelly slain by the fiend Grendel.

The harp is struck and ballads are recited. When the skald has finished singing of how Hnaef, the leader of a small clan of Dane-men, fell at the hands of Finn's men in a Frisian quarrel, and of the resulting blood-feud, Hrothgar addresses you and says, "Share with us one of your stories, Beowulf."

"Yes," urges Queen Wealhtheow, "tell us how you bested those Orkney giants."

If you want to grant Wealhtheow her wish, and recite the story of how you cleared out that particular nest of giants, turn to **307**. If you would rather not waste time on such vain boasts, turn to **192**.

### 202

When you come to fight the tormentor-worm, the Dragon, you may add 2 points when calculating your *Combat Rating*, and you may add 2 points to any damage done by the ancient blade Angurvadal.

Gain 2 *Hero Points* and then turn to **17**.

### 203

Opening the chest has triggered a trap. A mechanism hidden in the lid fires a dart at you, the tiny projectile hitting your wrist and remaining stuck there, until you pull it out.

The tip of the dart is coated with the venom of a sea-snake.

Lose 3 *Endurance* points and, if you are still alive, turn to **45**.

Digging not just one hole but a series of trenches is exhausting work.

Lose 1 *Endurance* point and turn to **226**.

## 205

Retreating a few paces along the passageway, you start your run up.

*Take an Agility test*; if you pass the test, turn to **241**, but if you fail the test, turn to **227**.

Alternatively, you may spend 1 *Hero Point* to avoid taking the test at all, and turn to **241** automatically.

## 206

You have also heard it said that Grendel carries no weapons other than those which his foul nature has given him, having slain the men of Hrothgar's hall with nothing more than unkind claws.

You judge yourself to be more than his equal in strength and fighting-prowess, so perhaps you should put aside your weapon as well.

If you wish to put take off your belt and lay aside your sword, turn to **186**. If you would rather keep hold of your battle-ready blade, turn to **164**.

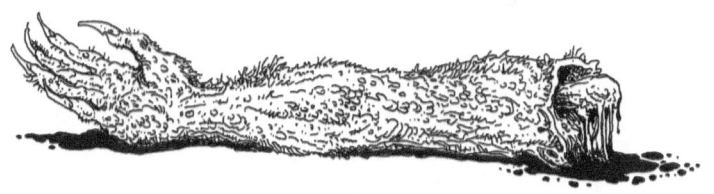

Despite straining with all your might, you barely manage to shift the heavy rock.

The giants' mocking laughter crashes down upon you like a landslide.

You sit down, sweat beading on your brow despite the chill wind blowing over the island, exhausted from your exertions.

You can only watch as your opponent picks up a boulder four times as large as the one you were trying to shift, with one huge hand, and with a grunt of effort hurls it far out of sight.

"You lose!" roars the brute.

Hefting its great stone club in its misshapen hands, the ogre thunders towards you at a lumbering run. (In this battle the giant has the initiative.)

ELADA THE ETTIN                  COMBAT 6        ENDURANCE 9

If you want to, you may spend 1 *Hero Point* to automatically win your battle against the giant (turn to **49**).

If not, conduct the battle as normal and, if you win, turn to **49**. However, if you lose, turn to **79**.

Muscles tensing, you attempt to leap over the cascade-stream.

*Take an Agility test*; if you pass the test, turn to **248**, but if you fail the test, turn to **222**.

If you wish, you may spend 1 *Hero Point* and turn to **248** straightaway instead.

The rush-lights suddenly flare and burn anew with a greenish flame. There is fell magic at work here!

Before any of you can do anything, Grendel bends down and grabs one of your host in his greedy hands. His hopes swelling at the thought of a gluttonous meal to come, the troll-born night-stalker tears the man in two, as you might tear apart a steaming chicken carcass. He wolfs down great gobbets of man-flesh, as you and your company look on in horror, gulping down the blood that pours from Handscio's veins and crunching on his bone-joints. Soon there is nothing left of your brave kinsman, the monster having eaten him whole, right down to his hands and feet.

(Deduct 1 from your *Crew* score.)

You cannot allow this malformed monster to live a moment longer! Shaking yourself from your stunned stupor, will you:

| | |
|---|---|
| Order your men to attack? | Turn to **229**. |
| Hurl a spear at the monster? | Turn to **249**. |
| Attack it with you sword (if you still have it with you)? | Turn to **309**. |
| Engage Grendel in unarmed combat? | Turn to **409**. |

## 210

Clinging onto the slippery rock-face with fingers hooked into any crevice you can find, you eventually pass behind the roaring wall of water. And there, overhung by ferns and framed by moss-covered rocks, you find the cave mouth.

It is dark within, but enough light penetrates from outside that, as your eyes become accustomed to the gloom, you see the opening is actually the entrance to a damp passageway. Where you would expect it to get too dark to see, patches of luminous moss growing on the tunnel walls provide just enough light for you to see by.

Do you want to enter the tunnel (turn to **410**), or would you prefer to jump into the lake, in search of Grendel's mother (turn to **335**)?

## 211

Although there must be a king's ransom in gold and jewels here, lying at the back of the cave, you choose an arm-ring of twisted gold as a reward for yourself for slaying the monster and his mother.

Add the Golden Arm-Ring to your Equipment List, record the kenning *Desire's-Slave* on your Adventure Sheet, and then turn to **231**.

## 212

And then, in your own berserk rage, you lay a mighty blow against the Dragon, the like of which only a hero such as Beowulf Beastslayer could muster.

If you have Thor's Favour, turn to **147**. If not, turn to **185**.

## 213

You have no idea how far down the lake-bottom lies – no man does! – but you swim on, deeper and deeper regardless, even as the pressure builds in your head and your lungs start to burn. But it is not long before your presence is detected by the one who dwells here.

That grim and greedy guardian of the flood, keeping her hungry hundred-season watch, glides up from the depths and you only become aware of her presence when she grabs you.

If you are wearing the Silver Corselet, turn to **183**, but if not, turn to **166**.

## 214

You have cleansed Heorot of its curse and saved the mead-hall, not to mention Hrothgar's people, from further persecution by the horror. As a sign to all that Grendel the bone-grinder is gone and Heorot is rid of its scourge, you hang the monster's mighty arm from the rafters above the door of the mead-hall for all to see.

Gain 1 more *Hero Point* and then turn to **382**.

## 215

Your body is imbued with the power that lies within the bones of the men you have eaten.

Gain 1 *Agility* point and then turn to **444**.

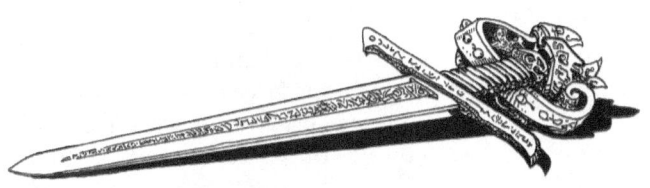

## 216

As you continue on your way through the forest, the strange cries fade into silence; the woods are not even disturbed by birdsong. It is eerie and unsettling.

Suddenly a wolf-howl cuts through the stillness.

The pack comes for you then, all slavering jaws, savage growls, and bloodthirsty intent.

If you have the kenning *War-Rage* written on your Adventure Sheet, turn to **187**. If not, turn to **157**.

## 217

Sword in hand, you wait for the Orca to break the surface again, ready to deliver a powerful blow and drive it back into the night-dark depths. And then the monster bursts from the sea, foam-flecked, its black and white whale-skin striking to the eye, and you prepare to strike. (Which of you has the initiative in this mighty sea-battle will depend on how you came to this moment.)

ORCA                    COMBAT 8        ENDURANCE 10

If you want, you may spend 2 *Hero Points* to automatically win the battle with the whale (turn to **10**). If not, you will have to fight it and only if you win, turn to **10**.

## 218

As the darkness and the water swallow you, the weight of your weapon and armour helping carry you to the bottom, you feel your way forward with your hands, soon finding the entrance to the sunken tunnel.

But as you pull yourself into the channel and start to swim along it, in total darkness, you sense a commotion in the water around you as something attacks. Needle-sharp teeth tear at your arms and legs, but all you can do is keep swimming, in the hope that you will emerge from the tunnel soon and escape the creatures that are attacking you.

Roll two dice (or pick a card) and deduct that many *Endurance* points. (Picture cards are worth 11, while an Ace is worth 12.) If you lose 6-9 *Endurance* points, you must also lose 1 *Agility* point and 1 *Combat* point. But if you lose 10-12 *Endurance* points, you must also lose 2 *Agility* points and 2 *Combat* points.

If you survive the attack, turn to **72**. If not, turn to **179**.


### 219

While your eyes and other senses are telling you one thing, a small voice at the back of your mind is trying to tell you another. It is telling you that there is something wrong here, and that what you are seeing cannot be trusted.

Casting your eyes away from the beautiful vision before you, it is only then that you see the skeletal remains of the monsters' feasting: the ribcage of a bear; the skulls of both wolves and sheep; and the half-eaten remains of Hrothgar's advisor Aeshere, the stones still wet with his blood.

The shock of the sight shakes you from your stupor. Looking up again you see the creature before you for what she really is – not a divine beauty to rival the goddess Freya, but a hideous harridan, with crooked fangs for teeth, long claw-like fingernails, and sparse strands of wiry white hair on her head. Her skin is the colour of swamp-water and she has the aroma to match. She would be taller than you, if she was not bent almost double.

With a scream of rage that resounds from the walls of the cave she attacks.

Turn to **288**.

The double-edged blade is so enormous that no other man would be equal to the task of lifting it and bearing it in battle-play. But you are no other man; you are Beowulf, champion of the Geats, and saviour of the Scyldings.

Shaking with war-rage, you catch it up by its rich hilt and, careless of your own life, brandish it about your head, as you face the sea-hag once more, a battle-cry on your lips and the oath you swore to Hrothgar burning in your heart.

Now that you are wielding a weapon capable of breaking the witch's life-preserving enchantments as well as her body, continue your battle with Grendel's mother – in which you now have the initiative – and, if you win, turn to **173**.

Alternatively, you may spend 2 *Hero Points* and turn to **173** straightaway.

Suddenly a foot slips and, losing your grip on the water-washed rock-face, you cannot help plunging into the churning waters of the mere.

You are quickly surrounded by the swerving, sinuous bodies of the lake's denizens. Unsheathing your sword, you slash the blade through the water, as best you can. (In this battle, it is the water-snakes that have the initiative.)

WATER-SNAKES                    COMBAT 7          ENDURANCE 9

If you want to ensure that you win this fight, you may spend 2 *Hero Points* and turn to **197**.

If not, you will have a real fight on your hands. While you are battling the water-snakes, because you are doing so underwater, you must temporarily reduce your *Combat* score by 1 point. Also, because you are having to conduct this battle whilst holding your breath, if the battle lasts for more Combat Rounds than your current *Endurance* score, you will drown. If you win the battle, turn to **197**.

## 222

Unfortunately, you don't have the required strength in your legs to carry you over the stream, and you land in the middle of the fast-flowing current.

Turn to **287**.

## 223

"Clearly you are a hero of brawn rather than brains!" Unferth snorts, and the Danes join him in his mocking laughter.

After all that you have been through, being derided for being unable to answer the drunkard's riddles still leaves you feeling like some inexperienced unbearded youth, and you worry that you have been diminished in the eyes of your men.

Lose 1 *Hero Point* and turn to **58**.

## 224

The numbing cold seeps into your very bones and your swim-weary muscles, fatigued by your marathon swim, can take it no more. You start to lag behind as Breca breaks away from you...

Turn to **308**.

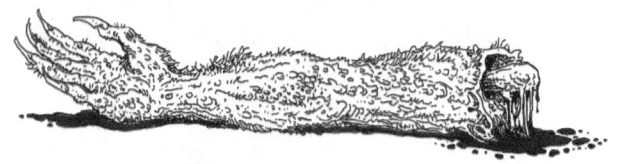

The *Sea-Wolf* is ready to sail with the morning tide, now that the storm has passed, but half your crew are still missing, after you tasked them with finding fresh food and water for your return journey to Geatland.

Dawn is still an hour away, the pink of a deer's un-felted antlers colouring the eastern horizon, when one of those you sent in search of food – Gunnar the Fair – staggers back into camp, bloodied and fear-gripped.

"Giants!" he cries, when he finds his voice again. "A tribe of them! They attacked us when we entered their ogre-claimed kingdom!"

"Where are your brothers?" you demand of the desperate wretch.

"All of them are dead," he says, weeping bitter tears for his fallen brethren.

Choosing four of your men to go with you, led by the heart-brave Gunnar, you set off in search of the jotunn-kin that claimed the lives of the rest of your warrior-band. You task those that remain with readying the *Sea-Wolf* for immediate departure, the moment you return.

You follow a gravel-banked river inland as the ground steadily begins to rise. You pass a joyless black lake, and a stack of rocks that rises from the rugged hills like still grey sentinels, until you come to a bend in the river. And there, lying broken on the blood-wet pebbles, their bodies having suffered the unkind attentions of stone clubs and axes, are the missing members of your crew.

As you stare in horror at the murder-site, your heart filling with rage at the dishonour that has been perpetrated against your men, five colossal figures emerge from the mist-shrouded moors on the other side of the river.

They are ugly, lumpen creatures. Where your men's honour shone through in their faces, the visages of these monsters are as hideous as their hearts are cruel. Where your Geatish warriors were men of noble bearing, these flesh-eating ogres are misshapen and grown beyond all natural proportions. Rough animal hides barely cover their ill-formed flesh, and in their hands they hold roughly-shaped clubs and axes of stone. Tusks protrude from their mouths in place of teeth and strings of saliva dribble from their gory jaws. They have clearly eaten some of your men!

You cannot allow this massacre to pass unavenged, but how do you want to punish the ogres for their transgressions? Will you:

| | |
|---|---|
| Order your surviving warriors to attack? | Turn to **188**. |
| Challenge one of the giants to a duel? | Turn to **108**. |
| Try to use cunning to outwit the murdering monsters? | Turn to **318**. |

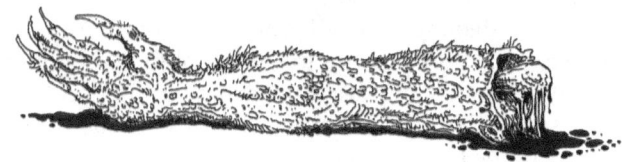

### 226

Having finished digging, you climb down into the hole to wait, with only the whistling of the wind to keep you company on the desolate heath.

Time passes, and still there is no sign of Fáfnir.

Do you want to continue to wait, crouched in the ditch (turn to **259**), or do you want to climb out of the pit and go in search of the wrym (turn to **372**)?

### 227

Reaching the edge of the rift, you hurl yourself across the void. But it is not enough.

Perhaps you misjudged the length of your stride, or you simply do not have the strength required anymore, but you miss the opposite edge of the chasm by quite some margin.

Weighed down by your arms and armour, you plunge into the darkness, where your body is broken on the jagged rocks that inhabit a sea-cave deep within the headland, and where sea-monsters hungrily devour what is left of you piece by piece.

Your adventure is over.

# THE END

## 228

It is clear that the ogress isn't lurking somewhere within this cave, and so, steeling yourself, you wade into the water. As you do so, you fancy you see the entrance to another tunnel, some way below the surface. But then, your motion through the pool sending ripples out across its mirror-smooth surface, your view of the tunnel is lost.

Seizing hold of the hope that you have found the secret entrance to the water-witch's lair, you take a deep breath and dive down, into the chill depths, heading for where you believe the tunnel to be.

If you are carrying the sword Hrunting, or you have Thor's Favour recorded on your Adventure Sheet, turn to **153**. If you have neither of these things, turn to **218**.


## 229

Screaming their bloody war-cries, your Geats charge at the ogre, laying into it with their swords and spears, and even their iron-rimmed shields. But nothing they do seems capable of penetrating its wyrm-scale hide!

In response, Grendel picks up two of your men and, swinging them about his head, dashes their brains out against the pillars of the hall; men you sent to their deaths when you should have challenged the monster yourself.

(Lose 2 *Hero Points* and deduct 2 from your *Crew* score.)

You can shirk your responsibilities and avoid the inevitable no longer. You must face Grendel yourself, but how? Will you:

| | |
|---|---|
| Hurl a spear at the monster? | Turn to **249**. |
| Attack it with you sword (if you still have it with you)? | Turn to **309**. |
| Engage Grendel in unarmed combat? | Turn to **409**. |

## 230

You are in the sea-horror's domain now and cannot hope to escape it. The death-fish seizes you in its crushing jaws and bites down hard.

Fortunately, your mail-shirt offers you some protection, but only some.

Lose 4 *Endurance* points and 1 *Combat* point. If you are still alive, turn to **160**, but if you are dead, turn to **190**.

## 231

Although the engraved blade of the Giant-sword is gone, eaten away to nothing by the un-dead monster's wound-sweat, you take the richly ornamented hilt, along with Grendel's head, from the monster's hall. Having survived the onslaught of your enemies, you also take up your own discarded weapon once more, before diving back into the lake, intending to return to the surface with all haste.

You set to swimming, striking up through the water, both the deep reaches and the rough wave-swirl thoroughly cleansed now the creature from the otherworld no longer draws breath.

If you have the kenning *Hero's-Promise* written on your Adventure Sheet, turn to **270**. If not, turn to **395**.

232

Striding along together, you and your men come within sight of Hrothgar's Hall at last. It is the most splendid hall under heaven you have ever seen, gold-adorned, its radiance shining out over the land. And it is to that shining retreat of kings you come, along a path paved with stone.

If you have the kenning *Dane-Friend* written on your Adventure Sheet, turn to **146**. If not, but you have the kenning *Corpse-Maker* written on your Adventure Sheet, turn to **46**. If you have neither of these kennings written down, turn to **273**.

233

Following the earth-cut tunnel, you soon come to a dead-end within the barrow. But there, resting on a carved, stone plinth, is an ornate dragon-crested helm. (Record the kenning *Battle-Hood* on your Adventure Sheet.)

It is a fine example of the armour-artificer's work, richly finished with gold and silver, and inlaid with precious gems that sparkle under the light of your torch.

If you want to put on the helmet, turn to **279**. If you would prefer to leave it where it is and return to the crossroads, turn to **328**.

Pushing home his advantage, Wiglaf makes a grab for the dragon-helm and pulls it from your head.

The moment the cursed battle-hood is removed, your senses return and you stare in horror at the Scyfling prince, recognising him again and realising that you were trying to kill him.

Even though you were not aware of what you were doing, you offer profuse apologies to the shield-prince for turning on him in your helm-possessed madness.

Lose 1 *Hero Point* and turn to **328**.

Alone, you make your stand against the ancient serpent.

And the terrible fire-drake has not forgotten your feud, as it comes for you, roaring its fiery fury to the heavens, its advance shaking the very ground at your feet.

Continue your battle with the Dragon, using the stats you already have recorded for the worm on your Adventure Sheet.

As soon as you have reduced its *Endurance* score by another 12 points or more, or after another four Combat Rounds (whichever happens first), turn to **212**.

If you wish, you may spend 1 *Hero Point* and turn to **212** straightaway instead.

"Come to me, my love," the maiden purrs, taking you in her arms and drawing you close. "My brave Beowulf."

For a moment you feel nothing but ecstatic bliss as the succubus wraps her firm flesh about your body, and places a kiss upon your neck. And then, in the next instant, you feel nothing but pain as something with the jaws of a hakarl sinks its teeth into your throat!

Roll one die and add 1. Deduct this many *Endurance* points. (Alternatively, pick a card and deduct its face value from your *Endurance* score, unless it is 8 or above or a picture card, in which case deduct 7 points from your *Endurance* score.)

If you are still alive, turn to **255**. If not, in revenge for you having killed her son, Grendel's Mother will devour you, down to the last knucklebone.

### 237

"A weightlifting contest?" The giant roars with laughter.

"Why not?" you say. You point to a pair of boulders; one is significantly larger than the other. "We will each choose a rock and then throw it as far as we can. Whoever's boulder travels the furthest wins."

This provokes more guffaws from the giant-tribe.

"If I win, you will let us sail away from your shores unmolested and we will leave these bleak isles to you and your jotunn-kin."

"And if I win," growls the ogre, "we will eat you all. You go first."

Approaching the boulders, you wrap your arms around the smaller one, which is still twice as large as your head, and, muscles bunching, strain with all your might to lift it.

If you want to ensure that you succeed in lifting the boulder, deduct 1 *Hero Point* and turn to **143**.

If not, *Take an Endurance test*. If you pass the test, turn to **143**, but if not, turn to **207**.

## 238

Your fur is still on fire! For every Combat Round that passes in the battle to come, you must automatically lose 1 *Endurance* point; this is on top of any damage King Hrothgar's warriors may cause you. Only when the battle ends will you be able to roll in the dirt and put out the fire.

Return to **158** to fight the Warriors, but ignore the instruction that you have the initiative in the battle; instead, the warriors have the initiative.

## 239

Even the collapse of a burning hall cannot stop the formidable hero-king Beowulf Beastslayer!

(Gain 2 *Hero Points*.)

Rising from the ruins, you regroup with your warriors and watch as the flame-red monster flies back to its barrow-cave lair, carried high on the columns of heated air rising from the burning village.

Everything is aflame around you – from your high-gabled hall to the proud stockade and settlement that surround it.

You cannot let such a heinous crime go unpunished, and so you set off in pursuit of the evil worm. But how do you want to approach its wilderness lair?

By sea?                                    Turn to **132**.

By land?                                   Turn to **175**.

## 240

Scrambling over the wet rocks, you skirt the edge of the lake, where the black cliff-face rises up from the shoreline, taking care not to slip and fall into the lake's icy depths.

Soon the roar of the waterfall is the only sound that fills your ears, and you are drenched by the clouds of mist-spray thrown up by the tumbling torrent.

As you approach the crashing cascade, you glimpse what looks like the dark mouth of a cave behind the waterfall. But the closer you get to the waterfall, so the rocks become more treacherous and difficult to negotiate.

*Take an Agility test.* If you pass the test, turn to **210**. If you fail the test, turn to **221**.


### 241

Sprinting for the rift, your courage screwed tight to its sticking place, you throw your old bones across the yawning gulf…

… and land safely on the other side!

Wiglaf follows you over, with a heroic leap of his own, having promised to stand by you until the end.

You set off again, along the tunnel, but before long, you find yourself at a dead-end under the ground. It looks like part of the earth roof might have collapsed in years past, but whatever the truth of the matter, you are going to have to go back the way you came, if you are to proceed any further through the barrow.

But as you do so, something that was hidden before emerges now, into the torch-light, ragged claws raised. It is another of the grey-skinned, withered-limb guardians of this accursed place and you have no choice but to fight it. (In this battle, the draugr has the initiative.)

DRAUGR                    COMBAT 6        ENDURANCE 7

If you wish, you may spend 1 *Hero Point* to automatically win this battle (turn to **297**).

If not, Wiglaf will join you in your battle against the risen corpse. Each Combat Round you will have two attacks rather than just one; if one or other of the attacks is successful, you will injure the draugr, but if both attacks are successful, you do double damage for that Combat Round. However, the draugr is focusing its attacks against you, so if it wins a Combat Round, you are the one who will come to harm.

If you defeat your opponent, turn to **297**.

### 242

"I thank you, my Queen," you reply, locking eyes with the radiant Wealhtheow once more. "I shall always consider Heorot a second home."

You drink deeply from the cup, and as the alcohol warms first your throat and then your belly, you feel strange forces working within you as you accept the blessed offering of Hrothgar's hall.

Add 2 points to your *Endurance* score, 1 point to your *Combat* score, and 1 point to your *Agility* score, and then turn to **333**.

### 243

Your frenzied attack is enough to discourage the water-snakes from trying to take you down again, and those slithering serpents that are still alive retreat to the icy depths once more, allowing you to resume your descent.

Turn to **213**.

## 244

Kneeling on the ground before the chest, you take the lid firmly in both hands and open it. You are barely aware of the click as something flies out of the chest straight at you.

If you have Loki's Favour recorded on your Adventure Sheet, turn to **184**.

If not, *Take an Agility test*. If you pass the test, turn to **184**, but if you fail the test, turn to **203**.

Alternatively, you may spend 1 *Hero Point* to avoid having to take the test at all, and turn to **184** immediately.


## 245

Removing your boar-helm and slipping off your ring-mail war-shirt, you savour the sensation of the weight of iron being lifted from you. You tense and relax your muscles, feeling that you will be able to move in a more supple way in the battle to come.

Gain 1 *Hero Point* and note that you are no longer wearing your armour. Now turn to **206**.


## 246

The trees start to thin out and after another hour's walking, you emerge on the far side of the forest.

However, before you leave the forest, you manage to forage 2 Meals' worth of provisions, in berries and birds' eggs.

The bleak and boggy moorlands stretch away before you, forming a dank quagmire in the shadow of the misty fells. If you are to reach your goal, you have no choice but to set out across them.

Turn to **258**.

Even one as feted and as lauded as you – for your great strength and might in battle – cannot lift the heavy blade.

As you are struggling with the Giant-sword, Grendel's mother comes for you. Eschewing her knife, she avenges the death of her only son with claws and teeth, tearing you limb from limb, and, when you are dead, sucking the marrow from your bones while your blood is still warm.

Your adventure is over.

# THE END

Performing a mighty salmon-leap, you cross the stream.

Turn to **32**.

Wasting no time, you seize a boar-spear from one of the weapon racks that stand at the side of the hall, and tensing your throwing arm, biceps bulging, you hurl it at the unnatural beast.

If you want nothing to prevent your spear from missing its mark, deduct 1 *Hero Point* and turn to **269**. If not, *Take a Combat test* and if you pass the test, turn to **269**, but if you fail the test, turn to **289**.

Taking the left branch, you follow the tunnel as it curves to the right and you enter a circular chamber walled with stone. On the opposite side of the chamber another tunnel leads away deeper into the barrow complex, but before you can reach that you will have to get past the guard who must have stood here, on sentry duty, through three hundred winters or more.

It looks like a warrior – clad in rusted ring-mail and with a corroded blade of ancient iron gripped tight in one hand – but it is also quite clearly a corpse. Its body is dust-dry, rid of all moisture, its muscles and sinews exposed as knotted tree-roots that wind about its limbs, while its eye-sockets are empty.

And then it speaks in a parched voice:

"Hwā besmīte þæs mihtigan eotenbanan, mǣran hēafodgrīpendes byrgene?"

Gif þū canst understandan hwæt se beorgweard segþ, wend tō twā hund.

Turn to **5**.

What started out as a youthful boast – how you and Breca should undertake a trial of strength upon the ocean – has turned into a terrible test of endurance.

You and Breca have been swimming for five days now, swords in hand, so that you might defend yourselves against whales and other denizens of the deep. But after so many days at the mercy of the wild cauldron waves and the icy chill, your muscles are beginning to tire.

If you want to ensure that fatigue does not slow you down, deduct 1 *Hero Point* and turn to **278**.

If not, *Take an Endurance test*. If you pass the test, turn to **278**, but if you fail the test, turn to **224**.

### 252

"I win!" you declare in your triumph, while Unferth skulks away to find a place to sit at the other end of the hall.

Gain 1 *Hero Point* and turn to **58**.

### 253

Following the earth-cut tunnel, you soon come to a dead-end within the barrow. But there, resting on a carved, stone plinth, is an ornate dragon-crested helm. (Record the kenning *Battle-Hood* on your Adventure Sheet.)

It is a fine example of the armour-artificer's work, richly finished with gold and silver, and inlaid with precious gems that sparkle under the light of your torch.

"Leave it alone, my lord," says Wiglaf the Worrier. "If this place is the hall of a deathless king, such a treasure is bound to be cursed."

If you want to try the helmet on, against Wiglaf's advice, turn to **279**. If you think your companion is right, and would prefer to leave it where it is and return to the crossroads, turn to **328**.

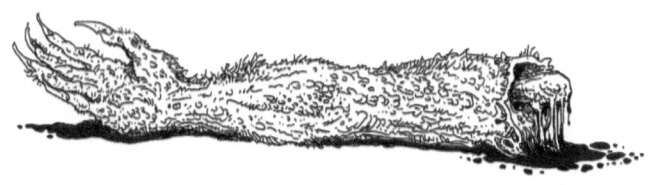

As you wrestle, the monster seizes hold of your skull in its terrible talons and, biceps bunching, bringing all its terrible strength to bear, rips your head from your shoulders.

Your adventure ends, murdered by the monster Grendel.

# THE END

Pushing the maiden away from you, you step backwards, stumbling with weariness, with one hand clamped to the place where she bit you.

You stare at the succubus in horror as the image of the elfin-beauty, her mouth red and glistening with your blood, flickers and shifts. The glamour she cast over you is broken, and you see the Queen of this damned place for what she really is – not a divine creature to rival Freya in her beauty, but a hideous harridan, with crooked fangs for teeth, long claw-like fingernails, and sparse strands of wiry white hair on her head. Her skin is the colour of swamp-water and she has the aroma to match. She would be taller than you, if she was not bent almost double.

With a scream of rage that resounds from the walls of the cave she goes for you then.

Turn to **288**.

## 256

Retreating a few paces along the passageway, you start your run up.

*Take an Agility test;* if you pass the test, turn to **272**, but if you fail the test, turn to **227**.

Alternatively, you may spend 1 *Hero Point* to avoid taking the test at all, and turn to **272** automatically.

## 257

You enter the hall then in a maddened rage, condemning the men that meet you in battle to death, by both tooth and claw, while they bring their swords and spears to bear. (In this battle Hrothgar's thanes have the initiative.)

THANES                    COMBAT 9        ENDURANCE 12

If you have the kenning *Sewer-Stink* recorded on your Adventure Sheet, you may reduce the Thanes' *Combat Rating* each Combat Round by 1 point.

If you manage to defeat Heorot's host, turn to **399**.

## 258

Under an overcast sky that forever threatens rain, you and your companions set out across the moors, beyond which you hope to trap the ogress in her dark domain.

After you have been travelling for several hours, amidst this bleak and barren moorland a figure appears. Your blood quickens within you, as you wonder whether you have managed to catch up with the mother of monsters before she has been able to return to her gloomy, lake-hidden lair. But as you draw closer, you see that the stooped figure is no ogress, but simply an old crone, bent almost double with age, draped in a cloak of black feathers, and leaning on a staff of twisted yew-wood.

There is something about the old woman's manner that unnerves you, and the reek of sorcery hangs heavy about her like a shroud.

How do you want to greet the crone? With wary words of greeting (turn to **285**), or with the sharp edge of your sword (turn to **371**)? Alternatively, you could just ignore her and be on your way (turn to **340**)?

## 259

You continue to wait, until you feel a tremor pass through the sides of the pit, and then another. It is followed by another, and another, as something large approaches your position. It can only be the monster that made the trail, the wyrm Fáfnir!

If you want to spring out from the pit to surprise the wyrm, with Gram in your hand, turn to **357**. If you do not want to diverge from the dwarf's plan and decide to stay put, turn to **330**.

## 260

(Record the kenning *War-Hasty* on your Adventure Sheet.)

"I have come from the country of the Geats to speak with King Hrothgar, not some coast guard," you say.

Eyeing your weapon, the look-out replies, "No one speaks with King Hrothgar without first speaking to me. Put away your sword and tell me your business here!"

If you do as he says, turn to **339**. If not, turn to **286**.

## 261

Fashioning a torch for yourself, you cross the portal into the earth. You walk quite some way along a tunnel shored up with large flat stones, the guttering light of your torch sending scuttling insects and wriggling things darting away before it, until at last you reach a junction.

Will you head right (turn to **281**), or head left (turn to **250**)?

## 262

You are quickly surrounded by the sinuous bodies of the deep-dwellers and lake-lurkers, and slash your blade through the water, as best you can. (In this battle, it is the water-snakes that have the initiative.)

WATER-SNAKES         COMBAT 7     ENDURANCE 9

If you want to ensure that you win the battle, you may spend 2 *Hero Points* and turn to **243**.

If not, you will have a real fight on your hands. While you are fighting the water-snakes, because you are doing so underwater, you must temporarily reduce your *Combat* score by 1 point. Also, because you are having to conduct this battle whilst holding your breath, if the battle lasts for more Combat Rounds than your current *Endurance* score, you will drown. If you win the battle, turn to **243**.

Twisting your body, you avoid the monster's grasping claws and cover the distance to the treasure-hoard before Grendel's mother can stop you.

The Giant-sword is a formidable weapon. Famed in former days, the edges of the mighty sword are worthy of a warrior's admiration. The weapon is a wonder of its kind, and yet it is longer than you are tall, having been hefted by giants in ages past. It is so enormous, will you even be able to wield it?

If you have Tyr's Favour or Thor's Favour, turn to **220**. Alternatively, you can spend 1 *Hero Point*, if you wish, and turn to **220**.

If not, *Take an Endurance test*; if you pass the test, turn to **220**, but if you fail the test, turn to **247**.

## 264

You may be old, but you are as fleet-footed as a man half your age.

Escaping the hall with your warriors, you regroup outside the burning building and watch as the flame-red monster flies back to its barrow-cave lair, on wings underlit by the fires left in its wake.

Everything is aflame around you – from your high-gabled hall to the proud stockade and settlement that surround it.

You cannot let this crime against you and your people go unpunished, and so you set off in pursuit of the vile worm. But how do you want to approach its wilderness lair?

By sea?                                    Turn to **132**.

By land?                                   Turn to **175**.

As the evening draws on and the rush-wicks shrink, Hrothgar becomes anxious, certain that the hell-cursed tormentor of his people will be approaching through the darkness, from his marshland home below the brooding fells, now that night drowns everything in shadows. At his command, the King's entire company rises, ready to quit the hall before the monster arrives.

Sorrow-aged Hrothgar turns to you and says, "Never have I left Heorot in the charge of another, as I do now, to you, brave Beowulf. I trust you will guard it well, and bend every fibre of your being and apply every ounce of courage you possess, to the matter of laying low our foe. And if you do indeed slay the beast, I hereby declare, before all gathered here, that I will show to you more generosity than any king ever showed to any man."

And with that, King Hrothgar and Queen Wealhtheow depart, followed by the rest of the Danes, until only Geatish warriors remain within the mighty mead-hall.

The hall seems eerily quiet after the carousing of the last few hours, and you feel the hairs on the nape of your neck rise.

"The beast approaches," you tell your men. "Let us prepare for its coming."

You have heard at the feast that the monster is a hideous troll-born ogre, a thing of scales and fur, wolf-fanged and bear-clawed. The fiend will come unarmoured. If you truly wish to test yourself against the monster, perhaps you should shed your mail-shirt before you face him.

If you wish to remove your ring-forged mail, turn to **245**. If you think it wiser to keep your armour on, turn to **206**.

You drop down into the stream, but soon learn that the current is stronger than you had been expecting. The torrent buffets your body, threatening to catch you up in its watery embrace and carry you away into the darkness of the fissure.

*Take an Endurance test.* If you pass the test, turn to **305**, but if you fail the test, turn to **287**.

Alternatively, if you wish, you may spend 1 *Hero Point* and turn to **305** straightaway.

## 267

"And I choose my club," the giant says, hefting its great stone cudgel in its misshapen hands. You assume a fighting stance, your wound-maker ready in your hand. (In this battle you have the initiative.)

ELADA THE ETTIN       COMBAT 6       ENDURANCE 9

If you want to, you may spend 1 *Hero Point* to automatically win your battle against the giant (turn to **49**).

If not, conduct the battle as normal and, if you win, turn to **49**. However, if you lose, turn to **79**.

## 268

You suffer your own injuries as you are thrown free by the Dragon's impact with the ground.

Roll one die. Deduct this many *Endurance* points. (Alternatively, pick a card and deduct its face value from your *Endurance* score, unless it is 7 or higher, or a picture card, in which case deduct 6 points from your *Endurance* score.)

If you lose 4 *Endurance* points or more, also deduct 1 *Combat* point.

If you are still alive, turn to **456**.

The spear hits the monster, and manages to pierce the flesh of its shoulder, penetrating between two fishy scales. Roaring in pain and anger, the torches flaring in response to its blood-rage, the monster rips the boar-spear from its flesh.

Turn to **449**.

The oath you swore to the dead warrior weighs heavy upon you. During your time in the domain of the fen-witch, did you find what he asked you to look for?

If so, you will have a number associated with each item; multiply those numbers together now and turn to the section with the same number as the total.

If not, turn to **395**.

Inspired by the golden banner they bear into battle, your warrior-band makes short work of the eel-like wave-lurkers, hacking their slithering bodies into bloody chunks with sword and axe.

Turn to **421**.

Sprinting for the rift, your courage screwed tight to its sticking place, you throw your old bones across the yawning gulf…

… and land safely on the other side!

You set off again, along the tunnel, but before long, you find yourself at a dead-end under the ground. It looks like part of the earth roof might have collapsed in years past, but whatever the truth of the matter, you are going to have to go back the way you came, if you are to proceed any further through the barrow.

But as you do so, something that was hidden before emerges now, into the torch-light, ragged claws raised. It is another of the grey-skinned, withered-limb guardians of this accursed place and you have no choice but to fight it. (In this battle, the draugr has the initiative.)

DRAUGR            COMBAT 6       ENDURANCE 7

If you wish, you may spend 1 *Hero Point* to automatically win this battle (turn to **297**).

If not, conduct the battle as normal and, if you defeat the walking dead, only then turn to **297**.

### 273

How many of the following kennings do you have written on your Adventure Sheet? *War-Hasty*, *Wave-Watcher*, *Raven-Feeder*.

None?                                Turn to **195**.

One?                                  Turn to **293**.

Two or more?                       Turn to **46**.

### 274

What reason can you have for not accepting the proffered goblet? What cause could you have for declining the Queen's ceremonial offering? In doing so, you dishonour Wealhtheow and bring into question the mind-worth of your honour.

Lose 1 *Hero Point* and turn to **333**.

"But, the gods be praised, I found a huge Giant-sword there, among her treasure-hoard, ancient and shining, and I snatched up the weapon," you tell Hrothgar and the assembled company. "And so I slew the keepers of the hall – first the mother, and then the son, risen again from his cold stone bed. The wave-patterned blade burnt away as Grendel's blood sprang forth, the hottest ever shed. But the hilt I took from the cave" – you indicate the hilt now lying on the boards before Hrothgar – "and thus I avenged the vile slaughter of your people. Now you may sleep in Heorot free from the fear that creatures of the otherworld might attack again – your company of warriors and every man, woman and child of your tribe, O Shield of the Scyldings."

With the demons' fall the golden hilt has passed into the possession of the white-haired warrior-chieftain, the Lord of the Danes, this wonder worked by Giant-smiths.

Hrothgar gazes long upon that relic before he speaks, for there, upon the gold, marked out in ancient runes, is the name of the sword, that finest of war-tools, with spiral hilt and serpent-bladed.

ᛒᚠᛏ ᛏᚠᛗᛋᛗᚱᚲᛗᛉᛏ

And when the King speaks, the hall is silent.

"This man was born to be the best of men!" Hrothgar declares, addressing everyone within the Hall of the Hart. "Friend Beowulf, your name shall resound in all the distant nations of the earth! And I shall make good my promises and reward you richly. But then I must let you return to your own people, across the whale-road, to the lands beyond the sea, where you will be a long-standing comfort and bulwark to those heroes.

"If only our former king Heremod had borne his great strength so peaceably! No, you are more akin to Sigmund, who, since the hand and heart of Heremod grew slack in battle, had of all heroes the highest renown among the races of men, in this refuge-of-warriors, for deeds of daring that bedecked his name."

(Gain 3 *Hero Points*.)

"But come, Beowulf," the King says, "take your place at the bench and rejoice in the feast, and in the morning we shall divide between us many treasures!"

Will you:

| | |
|---|---|
| Ask Hrothgar to tell you the story of King Heremod? | Turn to **145**. |
| Ask to hear more about Sigmund's heroic deeds? | Turn to **165**. |
| Join the feast with your men? | Turn to **89**. |

### 276

Strange cries echo among the black trees as you continue on your way.

If you have Wulfgar's Curse or the kenning *Blood-Curse* recorded on your Adventure Sheet, turn to **216**.

If not, roll one die (or pick a card). If the number rolled is odd (or the card is red), turn to **216**. If the number rolled is even (or the card is black), turn to **246**.

Alternatively, if you are able to, you may spend 1 *Hero Point* to invoke your heroic status by turning to **246**.

You search up and down the edge of the pool but can find nothing that gives you any indication as to where Grendel's mother might be hiding. It is only as you turn back towards the entrance to the tunnel, by which you entered the cave, that you notice the runestone for the first time.

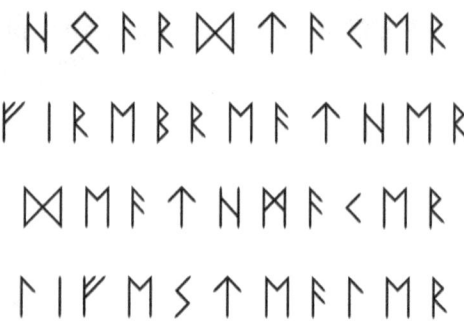

If you are able to solve the riddle of the runes, turn the letters of the answer into numbers using the code A=1, B=2... Z=26, add them together, and turn to the section with the same number as the total.

If not, or the section you turn to makes no sense, meaning you have got the answer wrong, turn to **228**.

Despite the cutting cold and your swim-weary state, you hold your own against Breca. He cannot break away from you, nor you from him, and so, matching each other stroke for stroke, you plough your furrows through the sea.

But then a storm rises over the ocean, with all the hate-fury of Hel herself. The North Wind turns its teeth against you, churning the waters and besetting you with the iciest of gales. And as the waters boil, disturbed by the storm, unfriendly fish-monsters rise from the ocean's black depths to consume you.

With a jerk of its blade-tail, a corpse-grey fish courses through the water, its dagger-fin cutting through the water towards you, its oblivion-black stare making it appear as sightless as blind Hodr. But it knows you are there nonetheless and in your desperate state you try to pull yourself out of its path.

If you want to guarantee that you escape the death-fish's savage jaws, deduct 1 *Hero Point* and turn to **64**.

If not, *Take an Agility test*, and if you pass the test, turn to **64**; however, if you fail the test, turn to **230**.

## 279

Having removed the helmet you are already wearing, you carefully lift the battle-hood from the plinth and lower it over your head.

The moment it is in place, you are beset by myriad ghostly voices, screaming inside your skull, demanding to know what you are doing, calling you "Thief!" and "Usurper!"

You immediately try to remove the dragon-helm, but, as you do so, the screams intensify, telling you that you are cursed, weakening your resolve.

If you want to spend 1 *Hero Point* to free yourself of the helmet's malign influence, do so and turn to **292**. If not, *Take a Combat test*, and, if you pass the test, turn to **292**, but if you lose, turn to **364**.

## 280

You make it back to the junction without anything untoward happening to you, but fleeing from phantoms is hardly the action of a brave hero capable of slaying an ogress.

Lose 1 *Hero Point* and then turn to **480**.

## 281

Proceeding along the earth-passage you come at last to a dead-end. However, lying there, upon a pile of dewy stones, is an ancient chest such as the artificers of your court would make, if they had the skill.

If you want to open the chest, turn to **244**. If you would prefer to leave it alone, return to the T-junction and take the left-hand branch, turn to **250**.

### 282

Unable to get out quickly enough, the roof comes crashing down on top of you in a welter of fiery embers and singeing cinders.

Roll one die and add 3. Deduct this many *Endurance* points. (Alternatively, pick a card and deduct its face value from your *Endurance* score, unless it is a 10 or a picture card, in which case deduct 9 points from your *Endurance* score; if it is less than 4 you must deduct 4 *Endurance* points.)

If you have lost 5-7 *Endurance* points, you must also deduct 1 point from both your *Agility* score and your *Combat* score.

If you have lost 8-9 *Endurance* points, you must also deduct 2 points from both your *Agility* score and your *Combat* score.

If you are still alive, turn to **239**.

### 283

The hag-fiend's talons catch your leg and gouge the flesh of your calf.

Lose 2 *Endurance* points and, if you are still alive, turn to **263**, as the ogress makes to rake your flesh with her claws a second time.

You hang on as, with great beats of its leathery wings, the Dragon takes to the air. Higher and higher it climbs, until the barrow is but a tiny speck on the headland, and you can see the smoke rising from the burnt ruins of your royal seat away to the south.

But as long as the worm is airborne, you cannot hope to bring an end to its life. For that to happen, you must force it back to the ground.

A sea-wind tugging at your hair, the misty threads of clouds dampening your face, you take your sword and as one of the serpent's wings comes within reach, you slash your keen-edged blade straight through the taut skin.

The Dragon roars in pain, and sends another cone of flame gushing from its mouth, but you are safe, clinging to the side of the serpent's neck, but for how long?

With one wing now flapping uselessly like an untethered sail in a storm, the ancient reptile plummets towards the earth. You see the headland rushing up to meet you and then the Dragon smashes into the ground, trailing smoke and flame behind it like a burning boat falling from the sky.

(Make a note that you now have the initiative in the battle.)

If you have Thor's Favour, turn to **456**. If not, turn to **268**.

"Greetings, grandmother," you say. "And what brings you to these barren moors this portentous day?"

"Hail, Beowulf!" the crone declaims, spreading wide her arms. "All hail thane, and king you shall be, hereafter!"

Thane, yes, and kinsman too, to noble Hygelac, but king? What can the old woman be talking about?

"You seek understanding?" she asks, in a voice like crackling parchment.

"I would know what you are talking about," you tell her sternly.

"Then let me read the rune-stones for you, and all things shall become clear."

There is something unsettling about this seeming seeress and you can almost taste the charms wound about her like a sorcerous shroud, but is she to be trusted?

Will you:

| | |
|---|---|
| Ask the crone to read the runes for you? | Turn to **300**. |
| Attack the old woman? | Turn to **371**. |
| Tell her to be on her way, and you be off on yours? | Turn to **340**. |

---

### 286

"My father was Edgetheow," you declaim, "famous fighter among nations. All wise men in the world remember him. And I am his son, Beowulf!"

"Then it is Beowulf, son of Edgetheow, who will feed the ravens this day!" asserts the Coast Warden.

"Aye, with flesh cleaved from your bones!" you declare.

With a shout, the warrior urges his steed forward, hoping to crush you beneath its hooves, but you do not intend to die upon this grey beach. (The coast warden has the initiative in this battle.)

COAST WARDEN          COMBAT 7          ENDURANCE 7

If you want, you may spend 1 *Hero Point* to ensure that you win this fight (turn to **316**). If not, you will have to conduct this battle as normal and, if you win, only then turn to **316**.

**287**

The force of the water knocks you off your feet, and you are carried away by the surge, before finally being tipped into the hungry darkness of the flood-fissure.

Weighed down by your arms and armour, you drop through the darkness, where your body is broken on the jagged rocks that cluster at the bottom, within a sea-cave deep below the headland. There, marine-monsters hungrily devour what is left of you piece by piece.

Your adventure is over.

# THE END

**288**

Whipping out your weapon, you prepare to meet the monster in combat. (In this battle, Grendel's Mother has the initiative.)

GRENDEL'S MOTHER        COMBAT 9        ENDURANCE 10

If you want to ensure you lay the first strike against the monster, you may deduct 1 *Hero Point* and turn to **338**.

If not, then conduct the battle as normal, and as soon as you win a Combat Round – if you win a Combat Round – turn to **338**.

Despite the monster being so large, your war-shaft misses its target, clattering from the wall behind the foul-born beast.

Turn to **309**.

You are slowly but surely gaining the upper hand as you continue to grapple with the bold champion. (In this hand-to-hand contest of strength, you now have the initiative.)

Continue your wrestling-match, remembering that if either you or the warrior win a Combat Round do not deduct any *Endurance* points. Instead, keep a track of how many Combat Rounds each of you wins.

If you win three consecutive Combat Rounds or you are the first to win five Combat Rounds in total, turn to **142**.

If Beowulf is the first to win three consecutive Combat Rounds or five Combat Rounds, turn to **83**.

The iron-headed dart misses its target and lands harmlessly in the water, breaking the surface of the black lake.

Hissing like a serpent, the sea-drake – with its bloated body, oar-like fins and eel-like head atop a neck as long as a longship's mast – makes the lake-shore. Dropping the bow, you are forced to enter the shallows to meet it in battle with your blade drawn. (In this battle, the sea-drake has the initiative.)

SEA-DRAKE     COMBAT 7   ENDURANCE 8

If you want to ensure that you slay the sea-drake, you may spend 1 *Hero Point* and automatically turn to **311**, otherwise you will have to conduct the battle as normal and, if you slay the beast, only then turn to **311**.

You tear the helmet off and hurl it to the ground. The experience has left you shaken, and doubting that you have the strength to complete what may well be your final beast-slaying quest.

Lose 2 *Hero Points* and turn to **328**.

## 293

A man, dressed in the fine clothes and furs one of the King's karls stands watch over the gates of the King's stockade, with the battle-brave sentries on guard duty there.

"I am Wulfgar, herald to King Hrothgar," the karl calls from atop the gatehouse. "What is your business here? You come clad in grey war-coats and masked helms, and bearing embellished shields, but do you come as friends or foes?"

You step up to the gate, spear in hand, your shield on your arm, and a hero's hunger in your heart.

"I am Beowulf, prince of the Geats, kin of King Hygelac, and if you will grant us an audience with your gracious king Hrothgar, we will explain in full the reason why we have braved the storm-tossed seas to journey to the land of the Danes."

If you want to invoke your heroic status now, deduct 1 *Hero Point* and turn to **363**.

If not, roll one die (or pick a card). If the number rolled is odd (or the card is red), turn to **391**. If the number rolled is even (or the card is black), turn to **363**.

## 294

Turning about, urgently thrashing your arms and legs, you try to escape the horrors by swimming for the surface. But the water-dwellers are more at home in this environment than you and soon catch up with you, one of them sinking its fangs into the meat of your calf

Lose 2 *Endurance* points, as well as 1 *Hero Point* for trying to flee from the water-snakes.

Now turn to **262**.

Waves of deadly flame come pouring from the Ravager's open mouth to envelop you, but you swing up your iron shield – no linden-wood strife-guard this – and the fiery torrent ripples around you, while you remain unharmed.

Gain 1 *Hero Point* and turn to **463**.

Noticing a half-eaten fish lying on a stone at the edge of the pool, you are sure that you are close to the fen-hag's home, but you can see no tunnels leading out of the cave other than the one by which you entered.

Do you want to continue searching the cave for any clues that might lead you to the ogress's lair (turn to **277**), or do you want to proceed by entering the pool itself (turn to **228**)?

The draugr dead, you return to the rift and easily cross the gulf, thanks to another powerful hero-leap.

Turn to **328**.

Pointing at the shortest of the cliff-tall giants, you shout, "I challenge you to a duel! You who set no store by mind-worth, you who defiled the bodies of my men by feasting on their flesh, you who are undeserving of a noble death, nonetheless, I offer you the chance to redeem yourself in single combat!"

When the booming thunder of the giants' laughter has subsided, the ogre you have challenged steps forward.

"I accept your challenge!" it booms, its voice the crash of calving glaciers. "Choose your weapon!"

Will your sword be your weapon of choice (turn to **267**), or, seeing several boulders lying in the river, will you challenge the giant to a weightlifting contest (turn to **237**)?

## 299

As you lay another vicious blow against it, the worm rears up once more, screaming its fury and pain. In response, the roof of the ancient chamber crumbles, and the earth that was heaped up on the headland so many generations ago by the men of that death-rapt race, comes down in a great flood of turf and stone, half burying the raging Ravager.

You cannot see yourself defeating the Dragon, trapped in a half-buried hoard-hold, and so while the serpent fights to free itself, you scramble up the hill of slumped earth.

As you climb, you feel the terrible heat of a fearsome fire-blast chasing you up the incline, but do you have the strength to outrun it?

If you have Tyr's Favour, turn to **366**.

If not, *Take an Endurance test*. If you pass the test, turn to **366**, but if you fail the test, turn to **341**.

Alternatively, if you want to ensure that fatigue does not slow you down, you may deduct 1 *Hero Point* and turn to **366** anyway.

## 300

"Very well," the crone says, stepping closer. As she does so, you are shocked to see that her eyes have been scratched out, as if by birds, and her eyelids are now just knots of scar tissue!

Squatting done on the ground, she clears a patch of earth and then takes a cloth bag from under her raven-feather cloak and empties a handful of smooth stones onto the ground.

"I see a watery hall and the wyrd-one waiting within, clad in a gown of glamour." The soothsayer pauses to wipe away the strings of saliva dribbling from between her black lips. "And I see an earthen hall, with one king kneeling before another, making an offering of gold."

Each of the polished pebbles has been marked with a rune, and laid next to each other the runes read:

ᛏ ᚠ ᚲ ᛗ ᛉ ᛦ ᛏ ᚱ ᛗ ᚠ ᛊ ᚢ ᚱ ᛗ

Can you interpret the riddle of the runes?

Turn to **320**.

## 301

Not knowing what other choice you have, you sprint for the far end of the cavern. But as you do so, the hag makes another lunge for you.

If you have Loki's Favour recorded on your Adventure Sheet, turn to **263**.

If not, *Take an Agility test*; if you pass the test, turn to **263**, but if you fail the test, turn to **283**.

Alternatively, you may spend 1 *Hero Point* to avoid having to take the test at all, and turn to **263** straightaway.

## 302

You have been bitten by the Varulfur and so you now bear its blood-curse.

Add the kenning *Blood-Curse* to your Adventure Sheet and then turn to **342**.


## 303

Then the Dragon comes, swimming through the night on wings wreathed in the flames that vomit from its mouth.

Longer than a dragon-prowed wave-rider and as merciless as a volcano's fury, the winged serpent descends upon your hall – that finest of buildings and gift-seat of the Geats – swallowing it in fire.

Grief strikes at your heart. What can you have done to deserve such a visitation? And then the words of the sea-hag echo down through the years to you again:

> *"Suffer the fury of fire and flood,*
> *And may the sea-tide turn red with your blood!"*

Spewing tongues of fire from afar, the dragon will not dare face you in single combat. The roof of your hall a field of flames, thick smoke rising from the rafters, the oaken beams burn through and the structure caves in.

Amid the screams of women and the shouts of your storm-warriors, you have no choice but to flee the burning hall yourself.

*Take an Agility test.* If you pass the test, turn to **264**, but if you fail the test, turn to **282**.

Alternatively, you may spend 1 *Hero Point* to avoid having to take the test at all, and turn to **264** straightaway.

The ghost-mist coalesces into the form of an ethereal warrior, and it does not take you long to realise that it is dressed in the same garb as the body lying on the floor of the cave.

"Who goes there?" comes the spectre's echoing voice. "Who would come to this demon-domain of their own volition while the blood still pulses in their veins?"

"I am Beowulf," you reply, "and I have come to kill the mother of monsters that dwells in this benighted place."

"Then you must be a noble warrior indeed." An expression of sadness fixes upon the phantom's face. "I came here with the same purpose, many years ago, but I was bitten by a water-snake and succumbed to its venom before I could kill the sea-hag. In my struggle with the wave-lurker I lost my father's broad-bladed axe and the golden brooch given to me by my wife. I cannot rest until I am reunited with those two treasures.

"If you are determined to delve deeper into the sea-hag's lair, and you should succeed in your quest, if you come across the axe and the brooch I would be grateful if you would return them to me."

"I will," you say, swearing on your life and your honour, before heading back to the junction to follow the other tunnel deeper into the caves.

Add the kenning *Hero's-Promise* to you Adventure Sheet and then turn to **480**.

You make it to the other side, without being carried away by the cascade, into the swirling darkness of the fissure-hole.

Turn to **32**.

## 306

You have slain the beast in its lair! Is this a sign from the gods that your quest to kill Grendel's swamp-witch dam will also be a success?

Your men celebrate your triumph with you, and you all feast on the bear's flesh. (Gain 4 *Endurance points*).

Taking one of the animal's claws as a trophy, leaving the rocky defile you continue on your way through the oppressive forest. The trees eventually start to thin out and then it is not much longer before you emerge on the other side.

The bleak and boggy moorlands stretch away before you, forming a malodorous quagmire in the shadow of the misty fells. If you are to reach your goal, you have no choice but to set out across them.

Turn to **417**.


## 307

"Very well, my Queen," you say in reply to her request, "but only because it is you that has asked."

You rise to your feet and the battle-boasts filling the hall die down, as those present, both Geats and Danes together, wait to hear your story.

"We were two weeks from home when a storm forced us to put ashore on the giant-haunted Orcades..."

Make a note of your current *Agility*, *Combat* and *Endurance* scores and then turn to **225**.


## 308

"So you are not quite the hero you would have us believe you are!" Unferth laughs, offering you a slow round of applause. The rest of Hrothgar's thanes join in mocking you with their derision-laughter.

You take your place again at the table, while your men sit in an embarrassed silence.

Lose 1 *Hero Point*, but restore your *Agility*, *Combat* and *Endurance* scores to what they were before you embarked upon your tale, and then turn to **345**.


## 309

Gripping your war-steel tightly in your hand, you charge at the brute-beast, ready to wrest its unholy head from its shoulders. (In this battle you have the initiative.)

GRENDEL                    COMBAT 10    ENDURANCE 12

If you are not currently wearing your ring-mail armour, any wounds the monster deals you will cause 3 *Endurance* points of damage rather than the usual 2.

If Grendel wins two consecutive Combat Rounds, turn to **329** immediately.

As soon as you win a *Combat Round*, turn to **349**. Alternatively you may spend 1 *Hero Point* and turn to **349** straightaway.


## 310

And it comes to pass, after Hygelac falls fighting the Frisians, and his son-heir Heardred, your cousin, dies in battle against Onela, King of the Swedes, the throne of the Kingdom of the Storm-folk comes, in turn, to you, and you become King Beowulf Beastslayer!

For half a century you rule your people wisely, defending them against attacks from Swedes, Frisians and Franks, while the oaths of friendship you swore with the Spear-Danes endure, until you have grown grey in your guardianship of the land.

(Restore your *Agility*, *Combat* and *Endurance* scores to the levels they were when you first embarked upon this adventure, and cross off any Meals you may have remaining from your

Adventure Sheet. If you wish, you may buy additional *Agility*, *Combat* and *Endurance* points, at a cost of 1 *Hero Point* each, up to a maximum of 1 *Agility* point, 1 Combat point, and 4 Endurance points.)

As the icy grip of winter seizes hold of the land, the Geats gather at year's end, and a great feast is held, in celebration of the occasion you became King of the Storm-folk.

Warm inside your hall, with all manner of meat roasting over the cook-fires, your people eat, drink and are merry, as your skald sings the Lay of Beowulf, relating your battles with the monster Grendel and his mother, and how you defeated them both in the shadow of the misty fells of Denmark.

Mead is drunk aplenty while the hall-servants parade great platters of steaming flesh before your table.

Which meat would you like to partake of?

| | |
|---|---|
| Venison? | Turn to **7**. |
| Boar? | Turn to **38**. |
| Salmon? | Turn to **66**. |

### 311

Driven into a feeding-frenzy by the blood in the water, suddenly the swarming water-snakes are on you, in a surging mass of writhing, grey-skinned bodies, and you and your men are once again fighting for your lives.

If you have the kenning *War-Rage* recorded on your Adventure Sheet, turn to **271**. If not, turn to **451**.

### 312

Blood pours from the wound in the wyrm's underbelly, soaking your hair, your clothes and your skin. And there is so much of it! It is a red tide that rapidly fills the ditch. But worst of all, with the dying monster's body covering the hole, you cannot escape as the crimson flood fills the pit to overflowing and you drown…

Turn to **479**.

### 313

"Enough of your questions! Take us to King Hrothgar!" you command.

Turn to **34**.

### 314

You slide to a halt right on the edge of the precipice. It is then that the Dragon catches up with you.

As the serpent emerges from the hole in the cliff-face, to stop yourself from being pushed out over the edge, you are forced to cling onto the bony protrusions that cover its armoured skin, and fight to maintain your grasp.

*Take a Combat test*, as you fight to hang on. If you pass the test, turn to **284**, but if you fail the test, you lose your grip on the worm's scaly hide – turn to **473**.

If you want, you may spend 1 *Hero Point* rather than have to take the test at all, and turn to **284** straightaway.

## 315

As your eyes adjust to the gloom, you see writhing shapes swimming to meet you from the shadowy depths of the lake. They are the same wave-lurkers that fled when you killed the Sea-Drake.

But they are no longer afraid. You are in their realm now, and they come for you with jaws agape.

Do you want to turn around and swim back to the surface to escape the water-snakes (turn to **294**), or will you draw your sword against the horrors (turn to **262**)?

## 316

The Coast Warden lies dead upon the sand. His horse has bolted and is already halfway across the beach, heading for the path that leads to the top of the cliff and home.

(Write the code word *Corpse-Maker* on your Adventure Sheet.)

Ordering your men to bring their long ashen spears and war-shields with them, you set off for King Hrothgar's fabled feast-hall, following the path taken by the horse.

Do you want to approach Heorot openly, unafraid of who might see you (turn to **232**), or would you prefer to wait until dusk before creeping up to Hrothgar's stronghold unseen (turn to **6**)?

## 317

You can just make out the ancient runic writing chiselled into the face of the stone. The runes spell out a message that reads:

*He who would steal from the lord who lies sleeping here shall suffer his great wrath.*

Wondering how things might have been different if Wiglaf's cup-thief had taken heed of this warning, you enter the barrow.

Now turn to **261**.

As you consider the drooling giants, with their ill-focused eyes and gormless expressions, you realise that you could probably best the brutes using the muscles in your head, as easily as with the strength in your arms. But which particular strategy do you want to use? Will you:

Challenge one of the giants to a duel?             Turn to **298**.

Try to start a fight between the giants?             Turn to **3**.

As you lay another vicious blow against it, the worm rears up once more, screaming its fury and pain. In response, the roof of the ancient chamber crumbles, and the earth that was heaped up on the headland so many generations ago by the men of that death-rapt race, comes down in a great flood of turf and stone, half burying the raging Ravager.

As the landslide comes down upon the Dragon, Wiglaf also disappears from view. But there's no time to search for him. The earth-flood will not hold your foe for long, as it twists its sinuous body and beats its wings to be free. And you cannot see yourself defeating the Dragon, trapped in a half-buried hoard-hold, and so while the serpent is distracted, you make for the surface, scrambling up the ramp of slumped earth.

But with every step you take, the twisted thing untangles itself until you feel the terrible heat of a fearsome fire-blast chase you up the incline. Do you have the strength to outrun it?

If you have Tyr's Favour, turn to **366**.

If not, *Take an Endurance test*. If you pass the test, turn to **366**, but if you fail the test, turn to **341**.

Alternatively, if you want to ensure that fatigue does not slow you down, you may deduct 1 *Hero Point* and turn to **366** anyway.

## 320

You have possibly gained a valuable insight into the future, but at what price? You ask the crone what she expects from you in return.

"Oh, nothing," says the blind seeress. "I am just happy to serve my mistress as she wishes."

"And who is your mistress?" you ask, and immediately feel an inexplicable chill in your bones.

"You will learn that in time," she replies mysteriously, "as all men do."

Record Hel's Favour on your Adventure Sheet and then turn to **340**.


## 321

Settling upon one of your mighty war-blades to take into battle against the dragon, the weapon-smith Weyland then sets to work with his whetstone, honing the edge of the already magnificent sword.

When you are engaged in battle, as long as you are using this sword, you may increase your *Combat Rating* by 1 point.

Now turn to **303**.


## 322

The savage beast-thing is dead. Before your very eyes, its corpse starts to twist and change again, until you are looking at a naked man, his organs opened to the elements by your cruel sword-cuts.

Turn to **342**.

You set about you, your iron-hard talons sending arterial-red sprays splashing across the walls of the hall.

Roll one die. This is the number of men you manage to slaughter in this way. However, if you roll a 6 you have still only slain 5 warriors.

Add the number of men you have killed in this way to the total of number of warriors you have taken out of the battle and then turn to **418**.

Tensing every muscle and sinew in your body, you will yourself to shake off the effects of the fen-hag's paralysing spell. Your determination pays off when you feel first your fingers and then your toes start to wiggle, and this is followed by movement in your hands and feet, your arms and legs, until finally you can move every part of your body again.

Staggering to your feet, you determine to finish the witch before she can use her hell-born magic against you again. (In this battle, you have the initiative.)

GRENDEL'S MOTHER        COMBAT 9       ENDURANCE 10

If you want to ensure you lay the first strike against the monster, you may deduct 1 *Hero Point* and turn to **338**.

If not, then conduct the battle as normal, and as soon as you win a Combat Round – if you win a Combat Round – turn to **338**.

"This was my intention in taking to the sea," you tell the Queen as you take the cup from her soft hands and drink deeply of the honeyed mead it contains, not once breaking eye-contact with Hrothgar's beautiful bed-fellow, "that I should once and for all achieve that which your people have long desired. I shall slay the monster Grendel this night, or in Heorot meet my end of days!"

"Your promise sounds as sweet to me as the song of the lark in the morning," says Wealhtheow, "and may the gods look as favourably upon your endeavour as they did so graciously answer my prayer."

Add Wealhtheow's Blessing to your Adventure Sheet and then turn to **265**.

## 326

Cautiously, you edge your way into the musty darkness of the cave. It is dark, but as you proceed with care, cold is replaced by an animal warmth, and the pungent odour only becomes more intense.

You hear a snuffling, followed by the sound of claws scraping on the floor of the cave, and then with a great bellow of a roar, a gigantic bear emerges from the darkness.

Rising up on its hind feet, the beast stands twice as tall as you and is a formidable predator. But it is one you are going to have to conquer, if you are to get out of the cave alive. (In this battle the Bear has the initiative.)

BEAR                          COMBAT 8        ENDURANCE 8

If you want to, you may spend 1 *Hero Point* to automatically best the bear (turn to **306**).

If not, conduct the battle as normal and, if you manage to kill the bear, only then turn to **306**.

## 327

A stream of fire comes pouring from the Ravager's open mouth and envelops you.

If you have Hel's Favour, turn to **348**. If not, turn to **370**.

## 328

Returning to the crossing of the tunnels, you fancy you hear something and see shadows moving in the darkness.

If you have the kenning *Wiglaf's-Warning* recorded on your Adventure Sheet, turn to **446**.

If not, roll one die (or pick a card); if the number rolled is odd (or the card is red), turn to **446**, but if the number rolled is even (or the card is black), turn to **497**.

## 329

Grendel picks you up, raising you above his head, and hurls you bodily across the hall. You come crashing down on one of the banqueting tables, upending the trestle and sending empty mead-horns and wooden platters clattering to the rush-strewn floor.

You are winded and your right knee throbs with pain.

Lose 3 *Endurance* points and 1 *Agility* point, and then turn to **449**.

## 330

Steadily the noise grows, as does the shaking that has seized the ground, as Fáfnir approaches. The overgrown wyrm crawls along the track, on four heavy legs, and spewing a cloud of poison before it. But you remain protected by your position in the ditch.

As the monster's great bulk passes over the ditch, almost blocking out the dim daylight altogether, you take Gram in your hands and drive the blade into the wyrm's body, up to the hilt!

Add the kenning *Wyrm's-Weakness* to your Adventure Sheet.

Now, if you have the kenning *Ditch-Digger* recorded on your Adventure Sheet, turn to **448**. If not, turn to **312**.

## 331

Splashing into the shallows, you and your storm-warriors prepare to take on the frenzied water-snakes.

If you have the kenning *War-Rage* recorded on your Adventure Sheet, turn to **271**. If not, turn to **471**.

You fight on valiantly against the ogress, and although you are brave in battle and fierce as a bear, you are in the monster's lair now, where her power is at its strongest and yours is at its weakest.

The hag is as impervious to your fists as she was to your blade, whereas you suffer the unkind attentions of her filthy talons, and even her snapping pike-sharp teeth, ten times over.

Roll one die and add 3. Deduct this many *Endurance* points. (Alternatively, pick a card and deduct its face value from your *Endurance* score, unless it is 10 or a picture card, in which case deduct 9 points from your *Endurance* score.)

If you still alive, turn to **301**.

The feasting continues long into the night, now that Hrothgar's company has nothing to fear from the fiend Grendel. But when his mead has been drunk, the King of the Danes declares the night's carousing to be at an end, and retires to his private bower with his Queen.

As the conquering hero, you are also afforded a couch in the King's house and so leave Heorot for the night, while your men and Hrothgar's thanes clear away the benches, each warrior settling down to sleep with polished shield, ring-stitched mail-coat, mighty helm, and stout spear-shaft lying within reach. It is always their habit to be ready for war.

Cocooned within a warm bed, sleep is not long in coming, but it is not long before your dreams of gold and glory turn to nightmares...

\*   \*   \*   \*

You are looking down upon those asleep in Heorot, as if you are hiding amidst the rafters of the hall. The rush-lamps have been doused, and the air is filled with the grunts and snores of sleeping men.

Only one warrior remains on guard duty, armed and sitting by the door, but sleep threatens to claim him too, his head nodding, until his raucous snores join those of the other Geats and Danes in their drunken slumber.

One of the great doors of the hall suddenly opens, with barely a sound, and a monstrous ogress creeps inside, the curled claws of her toes gouging furrows in the floor.

She is not unlike the fen-fiend that has been Hrothgar's curse for the last twelve years; only where he was tall and muscular, she is stooped and scrawny, and where he was covered with patches of thick fur, the only hair on this hell-witch's body is that which sprouts from myriad moles and the shock of white hair upon her head, matted and green with weeds and swamp-water.

The sentry on duty comes to wakefulness the moment he feels the cold night air enter through the opened door, but he is too late to save himself. In a moment he is dead – ripped in two by this unwelcome visitation – his death-scream waking the warriors sleeping in the hall.

Then are swords taken up and shields raised – while helm and mail are left, unheeded on the floor – as the banshee begins her brutal onslaught, shrieking like a mourning mother come to avenge her murdered child.

The ogress throws back her head, raising her eyes to the rafters, and seeing you there, with a grief-stricken scream utters a single word: "Beowulf!"

Turn to **433**.

"Ha! If you couldn't get that one, you are going to struggle with this," Unferth chuckles, pausing to belch before continuing.

> "Alone I wage war, wounded by steel,
> My master I'll save, though I'll never heal.
> What am I?"

The answer to the riddle is another simple noun. If you know the one-word answer, turn the letters of the word into numbers using the code A=1, B=2… Z=26, add them together, triple the total, and turn to the section with the same number as this final total.

If you cannot work out the answer, or the section you turn to makes no sense – meaning you have got the answer wrong – turn to **392**.

Taking a deep breath, you dive into the mere, the waves closing over you. With powerful strokes of your arms, and kicking your legs, you swim down into its lightless depths.

If you have the kenning *Deep-Dwellers* written on your Adventure Sheet, turn to **315**. If not, turn to **213**.

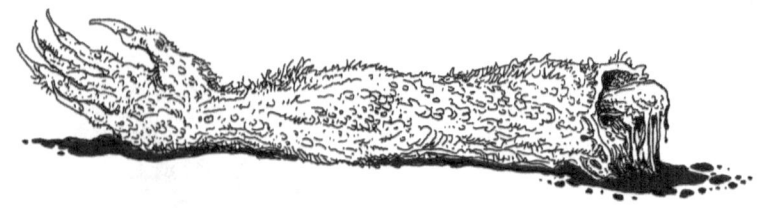

## 336

You howl in pain, your yellow eyes wide with pain and disbelief, as you desperately battle to break free of the warrior's grasp. But the young warrior clearly has something to prove, and is determined not to let you escape.

Reduce your *Combat* score by 2 points and continue your wrestling-match with the warrior, who still has the initiative.

If you win three consecutive Combat Rounds or you are the first to win five Combat Rounds, turn to **83**.

If Beowulf wins three consecutive Combat Rounds or five Combat Rounds in total first, turn to **37**.


## 337

"I slew five giants that day, your majesty," you say, finishing your story. (Make a note of this fact on your Adventure Sheet.)

"You are indeed a mighty hero," declares Queen Wealhtheow, "and once again I am reminded of how lucky we are to have had you come to our aid in our hour of need."

Gain 3 *Hero Points*, restore your *Agility*, *Combat* and *Endurance* scores to what they were before you began your tale, and then turn to **192**.


## 338

Not stinting the stroke, with such strength and violence behind it, the circling sword lands her such a blow upon the head as to scream out a strident battle-song of its own.

But to your horror, despite laying what you would have thought a killing blow against the hag, your blade – flashing like a bright battle-flame in the light of the shell-lamps – refuses to bite or hurt her at all!

If you are wielding the sword Hrunting, turn to **387**. If not, turn to **413**.

"We have come from the storm-lands beyond the sea," you tell the Coast Warden. "We are hearth-companions of the great King Hygelac and we have travelled the sail-road to seek your lord. It is with intentions loyal and true that we come seeking that glorious Shepherd of the Danes, for in our country the skalds sing of his feud with the marauding monster that makes vile spectacle of murderous massacres."

The watcher of the waves looks you up and down from his seat high in the saddle.

"I have not in my life set eyes upon a man with more might in his frame than you. You are no mere hall-servant, decked out with another's weapons and armour. Unless my eyes deceive me, you are a prince among men. You have the look of a hero about you."

"I am Beowulf," you go on, "son of Edgetheow, a noble sword-thane who knew your king of old."

"Then, if your sire knew King Hrothgar, tell me: who was Hrothgar's grandfather?"

How will you answer?

| | |
|---|---|
| "Scyld." | Turn to **352**. |
| "Beow." | Turn to **397**. |
| "Healfdane." | Turn to **374**. |

Parting company with the crone, you continue north while she resumes her slow walk south. But mere moments later, hearing the strident cawing of carrion birds, you glance back over your shoulder.

And when you do you can see no sign of the old woman – only a murder of crows, flying away over the moors.

Turn to **417**.

As you make it out of the hole onto the top of the barrow, the Dragon's fiery breath licks your back, and against the flames your ring-mail offers little protection.

Roll one die. Deduct this many *Endurance* points. (Alternatively, pick a card and deduct its face value from your *Endurance* score, unless it is 7 or higher, or a picture card, in which case deduct 6 points from your *Endurance* score.)

If you lose 4 *Endurance* points or more, also deduct 1 *Combat* point.

Make a note that the Dragon now has the initiative in the battle and, if you are still alive, turn to **456**.

## 342

You ride on over the moors, further and further away from civilisation, and higher and higher into the misty fells.

As heaven's joy turns the eastern sky orange, having crossed remote tracts of broken ground, following the foe's footprints, the outcast's blood-spoor leads you at last to a grove of dismal mountain trees, beyond which rises a wall of black rock. A waterfall cascades over the dark cliff-face into a boiling pool beneath.

This is an evil place. You can feel it in your bones.

Looking at the troubled waters of the lake, you see they are becrimsoned, death-daubed, boiling with the blood of the death-sick Grendel. There is no doubt in your mind that the fiend staggered back to his fen-lair and there cast himself into the pool, letting hell claim his accursed soul.

There is nothing more for you to do here. Turning your steeds about, you and your men leave the dark pool and its secrets to the water-snakes and fen-monsters and make the long ride back to King Hrothgar's hall.

Record the kenning *Dark-Mere* on your Adventure Sheet and then turn to **382**.

## 343

The *Sea-Wolf* sails on, but as the storm-clouds gather overhead and the sky turns raven-black, the sea-hag's curse becomes grim reality, as something terrible rises from the depthless ocean to ensnare the broad-ribbed boat in its unkind clutches.

Tentacles as long as a ship's mast rise from the white-topped waves all around you, as the Kraken wakes to fulfil the sea-hag's cruel prophecy.

Roll three dice in total. If the combined score of all three dice is equal to or less than the number of warriors remaining in your *Crew*, turn to **360**. But if it is greater, then turn to **435**.

You command Weyland the weapon-smith to make you a marvellous shield, worked all in iron, for a shield of linden-wood would be of little service against the fire-breathing serpent.

At last it is ready, and a mighty defender it is too, taller even than you, mighty hero-king, and bearing the image of the dragon you intend to slay upon it.

Add the Dragon Shield to your Equipment List and turn to **303**.

Hrothgar's gold-panelled hall echoes with the laughter of heroes, while the music of the harp fills the air and warm words are exchanged. There is much mirth and merry-making within Heorot once again.

Hrothgar's radiant Queen, Wealhtheow, rises from the King's table and passes through the hall, mindful of the courtesies expected of her, welcoming your Geats, this peerless, flaxen-haired lady.

She offers the mead-horn to her lord and master first, then to the old men, and young, sat at their benches, until she comes, her arm ornaments glowing in the light of the rush-lamps, to you. Her regal beauty rivals even that of the goddess Freya.

"Thank you, my lord," she says, her voice as soft and sweet as the lilting melody plucked from the harp's strings by the poet-skald. "I prayed to the gods to send us a man – a hero – who might be relied upon to aid us in these troubled times. They heard my prayer, taking pity on us in our plight, and sent us you from across the deep water-way."

She offers you the brimming vessel. "Here, bold Beowulf, join us in our toast to your coming victory over the hagseed-horror."

Will you accept the cup and drink (turn to **325**), or will you politely decline, having heard how powerful the mead of Heorot is, preferring to keep a clear head for the battle that is to come (turn to **265**)?

### 346

Can you slow your hurtling flight before you reach the edge of the precipice?

*Take an Agility* test. If you pass the test, turn to **314**, but if you fail the test, you cannot stop yourself before you pass the point of no return – turn to **473**.

Alternatively, you may spend 1 *Hero Point* to avoid having to take the test at all, and turn to **314** automatically.

### 347

Hrothgar's thanes are now fully awake and howling in horror to find you, Grendel Grimslayer, in their midst, in the gold-gabled hall. But they are brave men, and rush to claim their war-blades from the weapon-racks that line the walls.

Picking up a bench, from beside one of the tables that line the hall, you swing it in both hands like a club at the scurrying men.

*Take an Endurance test*. If you pass the test, turn to **405**, but if you fail the test, turn to **439**.

## 348

While the dread heat of the Dragon's blistering breath singes your beard and scorches the skin on your hands and cheeks, other than that you remain more or less unharmed. (Lose 2 *Endurance* points.)

You do not know what the Queen of the Underworld wants with you, but she is clearly not yet ready to welcome you to her domain of ice, snow and shadows.

Turn to **463**.

## 349

You lay a savage blow against the hag-born ogre, but it does not slow the monster for even a moment. You follow your first strike with a second, and once again your blade rebounds from Grendel's scaly hide as if it is somehow protected by some witch-wrought charm. Not even the truest steel can scratch the sin-spawn!

You stumble back from the monster, amazed and appalled. How can you harm such a thing if it is immune to edged weapons?

While you remain in this stupefied state, Grendel picks up an overturned bench from beside a table and swings it at you as if it were a war-club.

*Take an Agility test.* If you pass the test, turn to **369**, but if you fail the test, turn to **389**.

Alternatively, you may spend 1 *Hero Point* to avoid having to take the test at all, and turn to **369** straightaway.

## 350

Your long arms give you the advantage, and before the Danes can even get close to you, you slay six of them, your claws opening red-wounds in their necks and chests.

Make a note that you have slain another 6 men and then turn to **418**.

## 351

When you come to fight the tormentor-worm, the Dragon, you may add 1 point when calculating your *Combat Rating*, and you may add 1 point to any damage done by your mighty battle-blade.

Gain 1 *Hero Point* and then turn to **17**.

## 352

"Hrothgar's grandfather was Scyld, Shield of the Danes," you say, with utmost confidence.

Turn to **374**.

## 353

Using your claws to tear apart the wooden planks that form the wall of the hall, you surprise the armed men waiting within, with swords unsheathed. You set about you with slashing talons and snapping at the bond-warriors with your terrible fangs. (In this battle you have the initiative.)

THANES                  COMBAT 9       ENDURANCE 12

If you have the kenning *Sewer-Stink* recorded on your Adventure Sheet, you may reduce the Thanes' *Combat Rating* each Combat Round by 1 point.

If you manage to defeat Heorot's host, turn to **399**.

## 354

The sea-drake dead, the remaining water-snakes retreat at last, dropping from the cliff-ledges into the lake with a splash and vanishing back into the black depths.

Add the kenning *Deep-Dwellers* to your Adventure Sheet and then turn to **421**.


## 355

As Wiglaf falls, in one final desperate act, he reaches for the dragon-helm and pulls it from your head.

The moment the cursed battle-hood is removed, your senses return and you stare in horror at the Scyfling prince, now lying dead at your feet, slain by your hand.

Even though you were not aware of what you were doing, you have committed a terrible crime and an act of terrible dishonour.

Lose 3 *Hero Points* and note that you are now alone, and may no longer turn to the sections reserved for if you had Wiglaf accompanying you on your journey through the barrow.

Turn to **328**.


## 356

As you stand at the edge of the dark mere, peering into its icy depths, your attention is drawn to the thundering waterfall on the other side of the lake, and you start to wonder what secrets might lie hidden behind it.

If you want to negotiate the rugged rocky walls that skirt the lake, to examine the waterfall, turn to **240**. If you would prefer to dive straight into the lake in search of your quarry, turn to **335**.

The shroud-like mists covering the heath part, and you see the wyrm Fáfnir for the first time.

The monster is terrible to behold, as it crawls towards you, dragging its body low on four heavy legs, a body that is covered with armoured scales. And as it advances, with every reeking breath it spews out a noxious cloud of sulphurous gas that causes the plants it touches to wither down to their roots.

The creature may be slow, but it will be hard to avoid the toxic cloud that goes before it!

*Take an Agility test*. If you pass the test, turn to **437**, but if you fail the test, turn to **376**.

Alternatively, you may spend 1 *Hero Point* to avoid having to take the test at all, and turn to **437** immediately.

Pine trees, clung with webs and dew, crowd in around you as you make your way through the forest, heading ever northwards. Coming to a rocky defile, lying in the shade of a stand of silver birch, you see the shadowed entrance to a cave, tall enough to admit a man.

Could this be another way into the hell-fiend's lair?

If you want to lead the way into the cave, turn to **326**. If you would rather keep heading for the fells, turn to **276**.

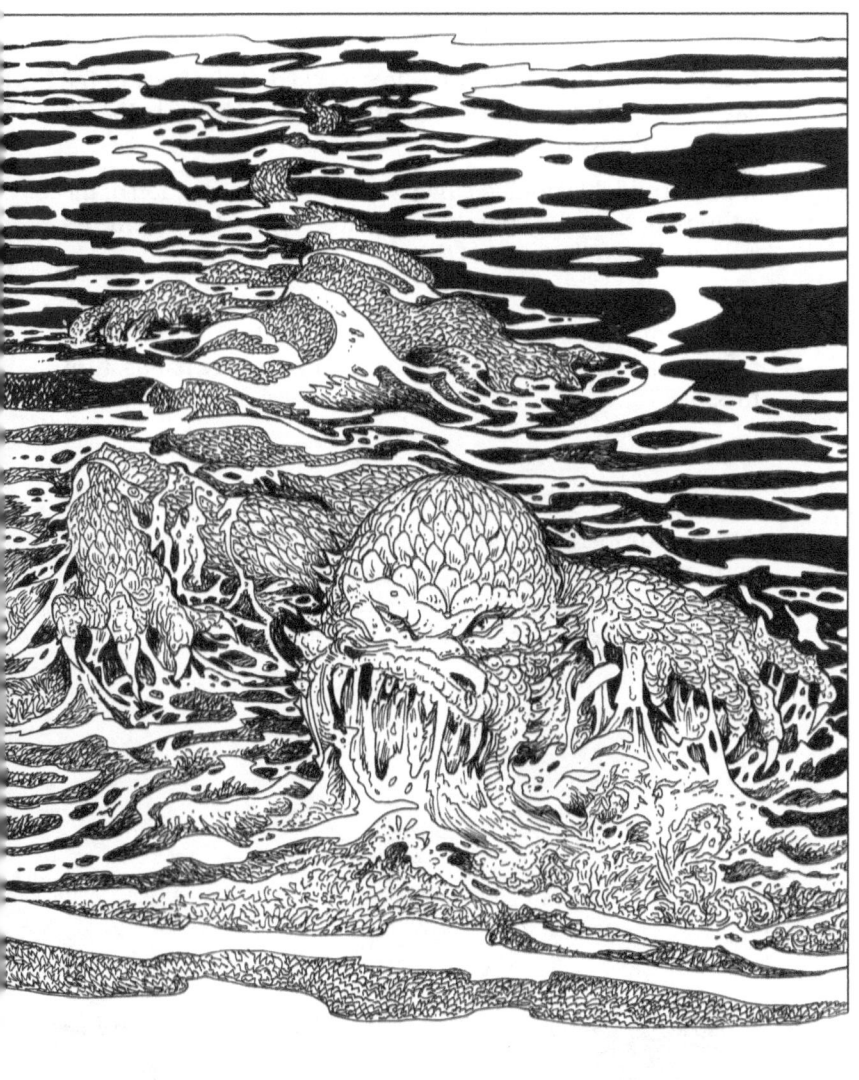

## 359

For the first time you begin to wonder whether you are capable of defeating the monster's mother.

It is then that among the treasures stacked at the back of the cave, you catch sight of a sword that might just be up to the job of killing the witch – if any weapon can!

It is a formidable double-edged Giant-sword, a creation of the jotunn-kin forged so long ago that the saga of the sword has become lost to the mists of time.

If you want to break off from your struggle with the ogress and attempt to recover the sword, turn to **301**. If you would rather continue to battle the witch with your bare hands, turn to **332**.

## 360

At your desperate urging, your proud storm-warriors pull hard on their oars as the storm-born wind fills the *Sea-Wolf's* banner-sail, and skimming over the open ocean, the wave-slicing ship escapes the squid-beast's clutches.

Turn to **36**.

"And what of Hrunting?" Unferth asks, jostling his way to the front of the crowd gathered to ogle the monster's head. "Did it serve you well?"

"Hrunting could not harm the hag-witch," you reply and see Unferth's face fall at your revelation, "as fine a weapon as it is. I accounted it formidable in the fight, a good friend in war, and thank you for the loan of it. But now I return to you what is yours."

Unferth accepts again the ancient heirloom.

Remove Hrunting from the Equipment List on your Adventure Sheet, but gain 1 *Hero Point*, and then turn to **275**.

Although your armour could not save you from injury, it did stop the Varulfur's great fangs piercing your flesh and infecting you with its terrible blood-curse.

Gain 1 *Hero Point* and turn to **342**.

"Then lay aside your spears and shields," says Wulfgar. "You will have no need of them here, for you will find only friends within King Hrothgar's hall."

And so the gates are opened and you are brought before the King.

His beard might be long, and the hairs upon his head may be white as frost, from the sorrow he has had to endure at the cruel claws of the monster Grendel, but there is still a sparkle in his eyes, and he still wears the circlet of gold about his head with the assurance of an honoured chieftain.

"Master of Battles, Lord of the North Danes!" Wulfgar announces. "King Hrothgar!"

The herald then addresses his lord. "These battle-companions have come from the country of the Storm-folk, borne from afar on the back of the sea, and the one who leads them names himself Beowulf."

"Beowulf?" says the King. "Beowulf is come here?"

"Yes, my lord."

"I knew him when he was a child! His father Edgetheow and I fought together. But I have heard the skald sing that now he is grown, he holds the strength of thirty men in each hand!

"Beowulf? Where are you? Come forward. Be welcome here."

Turn to **470.**

## 364

The screams intensify and your arms become weak, unable to even lift the helmet from your head, until, finally, you fall to your knees on the earth floor of the tunnel, your will broken.

You no longer even know who you are, never mind why you came to this accursed place, and so you will remain where you are, until thirst and hunger take you, and you become another of the sleeping king's undying guardians.

Your adventure is over.

# THE END

## 365

You have defeated an entire tribe of giants. With your fallen comrades avenged, you return to the shore, where the *Sea-Wolf* is already a-sea, straining at the leash of its chain to be away across the whale-road once more…

Turn to **337**.

## 366

The flames lick at your heels, but you make it out of the hole onto the top of the barrow without coming to further harm. At least, not yet.

Make a note that you have the initiative in the battle, and turn to **456**.

## 367

You can just make out the ancient runic writing chiselled into the face of the stone.

ᚺᛖ ᚹᚺᛟ ᚹᛟᚢᛚᛞ ᛊᛏᛖᚨᛚ ᚠᚱᛟᛗ ᚺᛖ ᚹᚺᛟ ᚺᚨᛊ ᛊᛖᛗᛗᛓᚺᚷ ᚺᛖᚱᛖ ᛊᚺᚨᛚ ᛊᚢᚠᚠᛖᚱ ᚺᛁᛊ ᚷᚱᛖᚨᛏ ᚹᚱᚨᚺ

Now turn to **261**.

## 368

You have a new blood-feud to occupy you now. Grey-haired Hrothgar and his hall company forgotten, you turn your fury upon the one known as Beowulf – the Bee-Wolf, the Bear, the Beastslayer! (In this battle, you have the initiative.)

BEOWULF                    COMBAT 10        ENDURANCE 10

If you win the battle with the warrior-hero, turn to **450**.

## 369

You dodge the monster's clumsy swing and, in his rage, Grendel hurls the bench the length of the mead-hall, where it lands with a crash at the foot of Hrothgar's throne.

Turn to **449**.

## 370

The dread heat of the Dragon's death-fire burns the beard from your face and leaves the skin on the back of your hands looking like pork crackling, while the smell of roast pig fills the hoard-chamber.

Roll one die and add 3. Deduct this many *Endurance* points. (Alternatively, pick a card and deduct its face value from your *Endurance* score, unless it is 10 or a picture card, in which case deduct 9 points from your *Endurance* score.)

If you lose 4 *Endurance* points or more, also deduct 1 *Combat* point. But if you lose 7 *Endurance* points or more, you must deduct 2 *Combat* points and 1 *Agility* point.

If you are still alive, no matter how badly burned, gain 1 *Hero Point* and turn to **463**.

Weapon in hand, you lunge at the wizened creature.

"Curse you, Beowulf!" spits the crone. Hissing like a hell-cat, she whirls her feathered cloak around, which breaks apart to become a flock of crows, her body seemingly vanished.

Rather than take off in a screeching panic, the murder of crows descends upon you and your men, and you are forced to fend off their tearing talons and pecking beaks. (In this battle, the murder of crows has the initiative.)

MURDER OF CROWS          COMBAT 8          ENDURANCE 7

If you want to, you may spend 1 *Hero Point* to automatically prevail in this fight (turn to **393**).

If not, conduct the battle as normal and, if you reduce the Murder of Crows' *Endurance* score to zero or below, only then turn to **393**.

The instant you emerge from the pit, you feel a tremor pass through the ground, followed by another and another, as something large approaches your position.

Turn to **357**.

Stepping through the door, you enter a hall fit for a king, but a king long-dead. Carved stone pillars support its domed roof, and a noble throne, carved of dark wood and draped with a sheepskin, stands before another door on the other side of the chamber, as if its owner might return at any moment, and take his seat.

But this hall does not resound with harp-play or the joy of skald-told tales. This hall does not ring with the voices of thanes emboldened by mead, or the protests of the women who are the unhappy focus of their attentions. For this place was constructed by a race now death-rapt.

You are standing within a grand burial chamber. The king that commanded it to be built lies upon a stone bed, clad in tarnished armour, his ancient sword in hand. But there are two within his hall who do not sleep, a pair of thanes whose duty to their king remains long after death has made corpses of them.

Moving almost as one, in their deathly duty, they advance towards you, as one of them issues a challenge.

"Halt! Who would dare disturb the eternal sleep of the King in his resting place?"

Turn to **8**.

---

### 374

The Coast Warden's face falls.

"Snake-tongue!" he shouts. "Deceiver! You have not come here as allies but as spies, come to see if the monster's raids have weakened us before launching a raid of your own!"

With that, the look-out turns his steed about and, kicking his heels into the horse's flanks, makes for the cliff-path again.

Do you want to try to stop him (turn to **98**), or will you let him go (turn to **78**)?

---

### 375

"I am Beowulf, King of the Storm-folk!" you bellow in response to the dead chieftain's honour-challenge, "and I am here to slay your dragon!"

Turn to **178**.

Despite throwing yourself out of the way, you are not fast enough not to be enveloped by the cloud of fumes. The touch of it on your exposed skin burns and you cannot help but inhale some of it, immediately breaking into a hacking cough.

Roll one die and add 1. Deduct this many *Endurance* points. (Alternatively, pick a card and deduct its face value from your *Endurance* score, unless it is 8 or above or a picture card, in which case deduct 7 points from your *Endurance* score.)

If you lose 4 *Endurance* points or more, also deduct 1 *Combat* point and 1 *Agility* point.

If you are still alive, turn to **426**.

"I have slain sea-serpents and even conquered a tribe of giants," you tell the King. "And so, just as Sigurd ended the wyrm Fáfnir, I shall slay your hoard-thief."

"Noble words," says the draugr, "and with a noble heart behind them. Having heard such a bold speech, I too believe that you can kill this fire-fiend."

Gain 3 *Hero Points*.

"But a dragon-slayer needs a dragon-slaying sword. Take mine," says the King, offering you his own ancient blade.

If you want to accept his generous gift, turn to **43**. If you would prefer to politely decline, turn to **73**.

You know the monsters' lair lies to the north, beyond the wolf-haunted fells, and so set off without further delay, taking seven of your most trusted storm-warriors with you.

Travelling north towards the lake's location, you eventually pass beyond the border of Hrothgar's kingdom and enter a lawless land that is home to wolves, bears and worse.

Far away you can see the black crags of the mist-shrouded fells, but to reach them you will either have to pass through a brooding forest, or travel across exposed and barren moorland.

Which is it to be? Will you take the forest path (turn to **358**) or head out across the moors (turn to **258**)?

### 379

You feel your body is re-energised by the battle-skills of the men you have eaten.

Gain 1 *Combat* point and then turn to **444**.

### 380

The Dragon will surely die of its wounds before the day is out, but you beat it into death's embrace, although you hope to be welcomed into Valhalla as a result of such a glorious death, even though there is no-one left to avenge it.

Your adventure is over.

# THE END

You swerve out of the path of the fire-storm, and then the flames die down again.

Turn to **422**.

The next day, the chieftains come from many leagues distant to see the arm of the tormentor hung within the hall, proof that the monster will trouble the land of the Danes no longer.

"Beowulf," Hrothgar says, as the two of you stand side by side, gazing up at the terrible bone-spurred claw, "best of men, I cherish you now in my heart as I would my own blood-born son. And you will be well-rewarded for what you have achieved."

The King's retinue brings forth from his treasure-house all manner of marvellous items. There is a battle-banner embroidered in rich gold thread. There is a mighty metalsmith-wrought helmet, a silver corselet, and a jewel-encrusted, rune-bound sword worked in gold as well.

But still the treasures come, as a team of ostlers lead eight warhorses, with gleaming bridles, into the hall. And one of the mighty steeds is saddled with Hrothgar's own war-saddle, studded with precious stones.

And last comes Queen Wealhtheow, bearing a torc of twisted golden wires in her slender hands.

"Dear Beowulf," she says, "take this collar. It is a Danish heirloom. Wear it and become as famous for your valour in battle as for your mind-worth."

You may choose three of the six gifts that have been offered to you: the Golden Battle-Banner, the Hero's Helmet, the Silver Corselet, the Rune-Sword, the Warhorses, and the Golden Torc.

Make a note of which items you have selected, and then turn to **402**.

<br>

### 383

A special sail is hoisted, bearing the image of the bee-wolf – the bear – and belayed to the mast, and the beams speak then. The wind does not hinder the wave-skimming ship as it runs across the sea, but the *Sea-Wolf*, with foam at its throat, furls back the waves.

But as you ride the waves, you hear again the last words the sea-hag's head spoke as she died:

> *"Suffer the fury of fire and flood,*
> *And may the sea-tide turn red with your blood!"*

How many of the following do you have recorded on your Adventure Sheet? The kenning *Desire's-slave*, the Sea-hag's Curse, and the Helruna's Curse.

| None? | Turn to **432**. |
| One? | Turn to **36**. |
| Two? | Turn to **467**. |
| Three? | Turn to **343**. |

The screams intensify and your arms become weak, unable to even lift the helmet from your head, until, finally, you fall to your knees on the earth floor of the tunnel, your will broken.

The spectral curse-voices fade at last and you slowly become aware of someone shouting at you, although their voice sounds muffled, as if heard underwater.

Slowly you raise your head and your eyes focus on the figure before you. He is clad in ring-mail and carrying a sword. You no longer even know who you are, so all memory of Wiglaf has taken wing, like an unkindness of ravens, and flown from your mind.

You only know that you have a duty now to serve the undying king who sleeps under the hill and so, getting to your feet once more, you raise your sword and attack the intruder. (You have the initiative in this battle.)

WIGLAF                    COMBAT 9      ENDURANCE 9

If Wiglaf wins two consecutive Combat Rounds, or four Combat Rounds (whichever is sooner), turn to **234**. If not, and you defeat your erstwhile companion, turn to **355**. (You may not spend *Hero Points*, on this occasion, to ensure you win the battle.)

"I have heard the name of Un-friend," you reply. "It is said that you have only wetted your blade with the blood of your own, Unferth Kinslayer!"

Your Geatish warriors burst into laughter at your taunt, while your challenger hastily returns to his place among the Danes, and says no more.

Turn to **345**.

## 386

It is time to enter the lake-lair of Grendel's mother, and you will go alone, as honour dictates.

"May the gods go with you," hoary Hrothgar declares, "and return you to us soon, safe and sound."

However, before you set off on your quest to deliver divine retribution to the wretched sea-hag, you must decide which weapon you will arm yourself with and what armour you will wear, for you cannot take everything you possess into the lake.

You may wear one helmet, one ring-mail war-shirt or corselet, and carry one weapon. Make a note of which ones you are taking with you on your Adventure Sheet. You may not use any of your other weapons or armour until you return from the lake – if you return.

You may not take any provisions with you either, as these would be destroyed by the water, although you may eat and drink before embarking on your lone mission.

Once you have decided how best to protect yourself, turn to **356**.


## 387

In your hour of need, the sword's-edge had failed its lord! The blade has seen many a battle, and has carved through the helmets of many fated men, but this is the first time it has betrayed its master, and its name. Is your enterprise doomed?

Lose 1 *Hero Point* and record the kenning *Wound-Serpent* on your Adventure Sheet.

Now turn to **413**.

The cave becomes a tunnel, a tunnel large enough to admit an ancient, fire-breathing worm. But as you head further along the natural passageway, surrounded by walls of stratified rock, you find your way blocked by a cascading stream. Water pours from an opening in the roof and rushes along a channel that cuts across the floor of the cave, to disappear into a yawning fissure on the other side.

To proceed any further, you are either going to have to leap across the fast-flowing stream (turn to **208**), or wade through it (turn to **266**).

You cannot get out of the way in time. The bench smacks into you, splintering across your back with the force of the blow, and sending you flying across the hall.

Lose 4 *Endurance* points and turn to **449**.

While you are enjoying your meal, the evening's celebrations are interrupted by the arrival of your cousin Wiglaf. He advances through the hall, kicking a wretched slave before him.

"What is the meaning of this?" you demand of the young prince.

"I beg your forgiveness for interrupting the night's festivities," the thane begins, "but I have dire news."

"Tell it then!" you command. You were never one to shy from dire revelations.

"This luckless slave has brought a curse down upon all our heads!" Wiglaf says, and casts a golden cup – a jewelled drinking-vessel the like of which you have never seen – at your feet.

"Where did you get this?" you ask, picking it up and marvelling at the craftsmanship of the gilt-smith who made it. (Record the Golden Goblet on your Equipment List.)

"Answer the King!" Wiglaf barks, giving the slave another savage kick. "Tell him what you've done!"

"There… There is a high barrow raised above the moor, my lord," the wretch stammers.

"And what were you doing there?" you demand, in a voice that is barely more than a growl.

"The sin-tormented soul had run from a flogging," Wiglaf interjects. "He hoped to flee and never return."

"I would have returned, master," the slave protests. "But as I say, there is a barrow-mound, such as the ancient kings used to raise. A narrow access leads underground. Seeking shelter from the ice and snow I felt my way inside. And that is where I found the treasure-cup."

"Tell the King what else you found," Wiglaf snaps.

"I did not know the treasure was guarded, but as soon as I realised that it was, I was seized with sudden terror and fled."

Engrossed by the runaway slave's tale, you ask him to elaborate further, pressing him for more information. But what do you want to ask him first?

| | |
|---|---|
| "What is this barrow like?" | Turn to **420**. |
| "Why did you take the treasure-cup?" | Turn to **438**. |
| "What did you find there guarding the hoard?" | Turn to **457**. |

---

### 391

"The gates of Heorot are closed to raiders from the sea," the karl replies. "And cursed shall be the warrior who tries to force entry. So say I, Wulfgar, herald to King Hrothgar!"

(Record Wulfgar's Curse on your Adventure Sheet.)

With a shouted war-cry, he and his battle-brothers engage you and your Geatish warriors in combat. You find yourself fighting Wulfgar. (He has the initiative in this battle.)

WULFGAR                    COMBAT 9          ENDURANCE 9

If you manage to reduce Wulfgar's *Endurance* score to 6 points or below, or if you are still alive after 5 Combat Rounds, turn to **93**.

Alternatively you may spend 1 *Hero Point* and turn to **93** straightaway.

---

### 392

It is no good; you cannot work out the answer to the riddle.

If you have Loki's Favour, turn to **430**. If not, turn to **223**.

## 393

The murderous carrion birds abruptly break off their attack and fly away into the clouds beneath the overcast sky, heading south, their croaking cries carrying across the bitter moors.

Record the Helruna's Curse on your Adventure Sheet and turn to **417**.

## 394

The chieftain of the giant tribe is not done with you yet. As you call on the gods to give you the strength to triumph in this titan-clash, the last of the ogres joins its chief, determined to put an end to you.

You must fight the remaining giants at the same time.

|  | COMBAT | ENDURANCE |
|---|---|---|
| BALOR THE BALEFUL | 9 | 12 |
| ANAK THE ACCURSED | 7 | 9 |

If you defeat your opponents, turn to **365**, but if you lose the battle, turn to **79**.

Alternatively, you may spend 2 *Hero Points* to automatically win your battle against the giants (turn to **365**).

## 395

Finally making it out of the monsters' lair, you return to the lakeshore only to find that the keen-hearted Scyldings and the kindly gold-giver their king have departed the cliff-head. Only your men remain, staring at the pool and sick at heart, until they clap their eyes upon their beloved captain once more.

Your company rushes to meet you, giving thanks to the gods to see you safe and sound. They quickly help you out of your armour whilst telling you that the wise men who watched with Hrothgar descried the blood in the broken water marbling the surface. Seasoned warriors, grey-headed and experienced, they counselled the King, saying that it seemed unlikely they would see the Geatish prince return triumphant, convincing him that the she-wolf had already done away with you.

Then, reunited, you and your warrior-band turn away from the lake, its waters sullied with the blood of monsters, and retrace your steps through the unforgiving fells, pacing the familiar paths back again, as bold as kings, carefree at heart now that your foes are dead.

Carrying Grendel's head from the mere is no easy task, and it takes four of your men to do so, bearing it upon a spear, and in this manner your storm-warriors transport your prize to the gold-gabled hall.

Turn to **412**.

### 396

How will you try to appease the furious revenant?

If you want to address the King by name, turn the letters of his name into numbers using the code A=1, B=2... Z=26, add them together, double the total, and turn to the section with the same number as this final total.

If you do not know the King's name, or you do not wish to address him in such an informal way, you will have to try something else – turn to **428**.

### 397

"King Hrothgar's grandsire was Beow, son of Scyld Scefing," you tell the watchman. "I seek audience with the great Hrothgar to tell him that I plan to kill his curse-monster, so take us to his golden hall at once! Lead us to Heorot!"

"You know of Heorot?" the Coast Warden challenges you. "Then if you are a true friend of the Spear-Danes, answer me this: what does the name 'Heorot' mean?"

How will you reply this time?

"Hall of the Bear." Turn to **415**.

"Hall of the Wolf." Turn to **434**.

"Hall of the Stag." Turn to **453**.

### 398

Selecting seven of your finest storm-warriors, you set off ahead of King Hrothgar's retinue, eager to trap the witch-fiend in her lair and put an end to her there.

Roll one die (or pick a card). If the number rolled is odd (or the card is red), turn to **258**. If the number rolled is even (or the card is black), turn to **417**.

Alternatively, if you are able to, you may spend 1 *Hero Point* to invoke your heroic status by automatically turning to **417**.

### 399

Nothing the Danes do can thwart you, the fell-fiend, Grendel Grimslayer! So you become the ruler of the night-hall, and Heorot is abandoned. The best of houses stands empty, missing the scop's song and the sweet sound of the lyre.

For twelve long winters you torment the son of Healfdane and those he is sworn to protect, visiting fierce sorrows and woes of every kind upon Hrothgar and his clan, and in that time you grow strong on your diet of man-flesh.

Roll two dice (or pick a card) and add the number generated in this way to your *Endurance* score. (If the card picked is a Jack, Queen or King add 11 *Endurance* points, and if it is an Ace add 12 *Endurance* points.)

Grieving songs sung by the skalds tell of how you have warred long with Hrothgar, as the clan-king grows grey in his dotage, turning your deeds into legends, and the might you wield into myth, spreading the stories far and wide, from the fjords of the frozen north to the rain-ravaged western isles.

And then from across the sorrow-dark sea comes one who would challenge your position as ruler of the night and the dark domains of Denmark, and once-silent Heorot resounds again with the sound of song, the clamour of carousing, and the bellows of mead-boasts.

The mirthful uproar grows louder and louder until you can bear the cacophonous chants of the hall-lords no longer, and you rise from your lake-lair.

Gliding through the shadows you come, the night-walker, until you stand at Heorot's door, when the furore of feasting has died down, and with a roar of rage you smash your way in, as you first did all those years before.

Half-asleep at his post, a sentry lies slumped in his seat by the door. But at the far end of the hall, wearing no armour and bearing no blade, is the mighty prince who has come to the gold-gabled hall to claim the blood-price for bringing to an end your feud with grey-haired Hrothgar.

Will you seize the sleeping sentry, who is guilty of the dereliction of his duty by the door (turn to **431**), or will you focus your attention on the one who stands, taunting you, from the far end of the hall (turn to **489**)?

## 400

As the blood pours from the fatal wound, in your hour of need, your faithful shield-prince is suddenly there again, at your side, and with a scream of grief-born rage he thrusts the tip of his blade between the Dragon's scales, and the flames rising in its throat slacken and die.

In that moment's respite you take command of your wits once more. Your grip on your sword like steel again, but still trapped in the monster's mouth, you thrust the blade into the Dragon's skull, driving the spark of life from it.

And so, you, King Beowulf Beastslayer, and Wiglaf, Prince of the Scylfings, make an end of the Ravager.

But this great accomplishment is to be the last victory in a long life of daring deeds. For the wound the fire-drake inflicted upon you begins to burn and swell, as the foul worm's fiery venom takes effect and burns you up from inside. You feel the bane begin to boil in your chest and know that you have come, at last, to the end of the allotted days of your earthly happiness.

Your most excellent thane washes your bloodied body and, sated with battle, you unfasten your helmet.

Through the pain, sensing that death is near, you speak: "I have guarded the Geats for half a century, and in all that time not a single ruler of all the neighbouring nations has dared affront me with his friends in war. But, wise Wiglaf, you must attend to our people's needs from henceforth. My time on this earth is done.

"Bid my men of battle build me a tomb, like this ancient barrow, on the foreland by the sea, that shall stand as a memorial to me, so that those ocean travellers who approach our Geatish shores shall afterwards know it as the barrow of Beowulf the Bear. Beowulf the Battle-king. Beowulf Beastslayer."

Removing the items of your office, you pass your gold-plated helmet, harness and arm-rings to the young prince, saying, "You are the last of our kindred. Fate has lured each member of my family to his predestined end, and now I must follow them."

And those are the final words you speak, before the choosers of the slain descend on their cloud-pounding sky-steeds to carry your soul to Valhalla.

In due course, your body is sacrificed to the flames of the funeral-pyre, and there is much mourning and misery among the people of your kingdom.

But your name lives on, passing into legend, as the mighty deeds you performed in life become myth, and part of a tale that will be told a thousand thousand times for a thousand years and more. The saga of Beowulf Beastslayer!

# THE END

## 401

Loki might be known as the Trickster, and a gender-changing mother of monsters, but he is also a conjuror of illusions.

Your dreams are filled with visions of the future – ducking the sweeping claws of a hideous she-fiend, opening an ancient chest, and proffering a golden cup to the corpse of a king – but do they tell the truth or are they lies, and how are you supposed to determine the difference?

But no matter what scrapes the legends say Loki got himself into, somehow he was always able to get out of them again.

Record Loki's Favour on your Adventure Sheet add 1 to your *Agility* score and make a note that you may ignore the next injury you sustain.

Turn to **427**.

## 402

King Hrothgar and Queen Wealhtheow have been beyond generous in the priceless treasures they have bestowed upon you. To find out more about the artefacts you have chosen, turn to the section number listed beside each one (but only the ones you have chosen).

The Golden Battle-Banner — Turn to **181**.

The Hero's Helmet — Turn to **71**.

The Silver Corselet — Turn to **91**.

The Rune-Sword — Turn to **111**.

The Warhorses — Turn to **131**.

The Golden Torc — Turn to **161**.

When you are done, turn to **201**.

## 403

The Dragon suddenly breaks off from the fight, rearing up on its hind-legs, spreading its wings wide. Its great horned head scrapes the roof of the chamber sending blocks of stone crashing to the floor. You start to wonder if the worm might bring the entire barrow down on top of you.

Do you want to continue to battle the Dragon inside the hoard-hall (turn to **419**), or do you want to try to lure the worm outside (turn to **452**)?

## 404

As the last of the colony leaves the cave, you turn your attention to finding a way to enter the ogress's lair.

Turn to **296**.

The bench sends another six of Hrothgar's liege-lords flying across the hall, taking them out of the fight.

Make a note that you have dealt with another 6 warriors and turn to **475**.

You share meat and drink, Geats and Danes together, filling your bellies with the first hot food you have enjoyed since leaving your sea-distant homeland. Your brave warriors share stories with the men of Hrothgar's dwindled company while you merely listen, and laughter echoes from the beams of great Heorot, the night-stalker that lurks in the borderlands all but forgotten.

(Add 4 *Endurance* points.)

"Beowulf," King Hrothgar's voice rings out across the hall, "tell us about one of your great exploits, about the heroic deeds you have performed, for just to hear such a story would fill our hearts with hope and happiness."

"As you wish, my lord," you reply, "but which story would cheer your heart the most? Would you hear of how I bested a tribe of giants in the Orkneys? Or would you prefer I tell how, one night, I fought and killed a bed of fin-backed water-demons?"

"Tell us about your contest with Breca!" a voice calls over the hubbub from among Hrothgar's warriors. "For I have heard tell how a certain Beowulf challenged Breca to a swimming race. Are you not that same Beowulf?"

"I am," you reply coldly, every muscle in your body tensing.

"I have heard that to win a proud boast you risked your very lives upon the fathomless waters, beating the waves with your arms while the sea surged with winter-spume. How you laboured for seven days and nights, only for you to lose the race. Breca was the greater, the dawn finding him washed up on the coast of Norway. And where were you? I see little hope of you besting Grendel if you cannot even win a simple swimming race."

"Might I know the name of the man who would cast aspersions upon the name of Beowulf, son of Edgetheow?" you demand, looking around the hall

"I am Unferth," replies your challenger, rising to his feet.

Will you rise to Unferth's bait and set the record straight by telling those present what really happened in the swimming match (turn to **481**), or will you ignore this sallow-skinned drunkard, knowing that your encounter with Grendel will be proof enough of your might and heroic status (turn to **385**)?

**407**

"Its edge is iron, hardened in the forge with venom, and tempered in blood," Unferth explains. "In battle it has never failed any hero who wielded it against his foes, and I offer it now to the better swordsman."

"And I thank you, friend Unferth," you reply, taking the proffered sword from the Dane.

Drawing the blade from its scabbard, you marvel at the artistry that has gone into making this wave-patterned blade of rare hardness.

"I declare that with this venom-tooth I shall slay the hag that has brought such misery upon King Hrothgar's house."

Record the sword Hrunting in the Equipment box on your Adventure Sheet and make a note of the fact that if you use the weapon in battle you may add 1 point to any damage you do to an opponent, due to its venom-hardened nature.

Now turn to **386**.

## 408

You are caught by the furnace-roar, against which your ring-mail offers little protection.

Roll one die and add 1. Deduct this many *Endurance* points. (Alternatively, pick a card and deduct its face value from your *Endurance* score, unless it is 8 or higher, or a picture card, in which case deduct 7 points from your *Endurance* score.)

If you lose 4 *Endurance* points or more, also deduct 1 *Combat* point.

If you are still alive, turn to **422**.


## 409

His jaws still dripping with the viscera of the young warrior, Grendel reaches out to seize you. But you are too fast for the monster and grab hold of that sickening hand.

The evil one is wide-eyed with surprise, realising in that instant that he has not met any man with so strong a hand-grasp as you before. And so you start to wrestle with the monster. (In this wrestling-match, you have the initiative.)

GRENDEL                    COMBAT 10      ENDURANCE 12

Conduct the wrestling-match as you would any other battle, but if you or the monster win a Combat Round do not deduct any *Endurance* points from the loser of that Combat Round; instead, keep a track of how many Combat Rounds each of you wins.

If you win two consecutive Combat Rounds or you are the first to win four Combat Rounds, turn to **429**. Alternatively, you may spend 1 *Hero Point* and turn to **429** straightaway.

If Grendel is the first to win two consecutive Combat Rounds or four Combat Rounds in total, turn to **329**.

The tunnel is large enough for you to make your way along it without having to duck, and you find yourself wondering if this was the route by which Grendel made his way in and out of the monsters' lair.

You have not gone very far when the tunnel branches. If you want to follow the spur-passage to the left, turn to **440**. If you would rather continue along what appears to be the main tunnel, turn to **480**.

Which sword have you chosen to wield in battle? If it is your trusted sword Naegling, turn to **351**. If you have chosen a dragon-slaying sword, you will know its name; turn the name into numbers using the code A=1, B=2… Z=26, add them together, double the total, and turn to the section with the same number as this final total. If you have chosen another sword, turn to **17**.

And so, at last, your bold Geats march back into King Hrothgar's hall, curse-free Heorot, while his thanes are supping, with you, their lord, standing tall with your head held high. For you are one who has dared to attempt incredible deeds and, having accomplished them, is now adorned with their glory.

You present yourself before Hrothgar, and there is much rejoicing as the monster's head, held up by its lank locks, is manhandled into the mead-hall where the Danes are quaffing their master's mead. It is an ugly thing for Hrothgar's karls and his Queen to behold, but an awesome sight nonetheless.

"Behold!" you say, casting the hilt of the Giant-sword at the foot of the King's dais. "What you see here, O son of Healfdane, prince of the Scyldings, it was a pleasure to bring to your hall. For these tokens – this head and this hilt – are trophies, taken from the lake, as proof of the victory I have won over the monsters that festered there."

The King and his thanes applaud your efforts.

"Nor did I easily survive the fight under the dark mere," you go on. "I performed this deed not without a struggle, I assure you."

If you have the kenning *Wound-Serpent* recorded on your Adventure Sheet, turn to **361**. If not, turn to **275**.

### 413

Determined not to let your sword's failure stop you from defeating the mother of monsters, you renew your courage. After all, you defeated Grendel by tearing off his arm with your bare hands, in your bear-possessed berserker rage!

Still intent on killing the monster's mother, in your fury you fling the weapon to the ground – spiral-patterned, precious in its clasps, stiff and steel-edged. Your own strength will suffice – the might of your hands!

Leaping at her, you seize the hideous hag by the shoulder, intending to do to her what you did to her son.

*Take a Combat test.* If you pass the test, turn to **443**, but if you fail the test, turn to **461**.

If you want to spend 1 *Hero Point*, rather than have to take the test, do so and turn to **443**.

### 414

Selecting seven of your finest storm-warriors, you climb into the saddle of the stallion Alsvior, while the rest mount the remaining warhorses you were given by the King. Not waiting for Hrothgar's retinue to finish readying themselves, the eight of you set off at a gallop, seeking the witch-fiend's lake-lair.

Turn to **417**.

### 415

"Heorot means 'Hall of the Bear'," you say, "and I have heard that the mead served within its walls was as sweet as the sweetest honey any bear could ever hope to forage."

Turn to **374**.

## 416

The King is dead! Long live the King!

He who lay sleeping beneath the barrow is now just mouldering bones and tattered, tarnished ring-mail.

However, there is one thing in the dead draugr's possession that may be of interest to you. Still clutched in one hand – a hand that has become separated from the rest of the body – is the dead King's sword.

If you want to take the sword, turn to **43**. If not, turn to **105**.

## 417

Leaving the fog-bound moors at last, you make your way by steep scree-slopes and scant tracks – where your party is forced to walk in single file – until at long last, the trail you are following leads you up over broken, rocky ground to a grove of dismal ash-trees, beyond which rises a wall of black rock. There a waterfall thunders over the rock-face into a boiling pool below.

The water beneath is turbid with blood. But worse by far is the sight of the head of Hrothgar's noble counsellor, Aeshere, resting at the edge of the cliff.

You are not alone in this accursed place. Drawn by the blood in the water, lake-dwellers have come to the surface, a multitude of writhing and thrashing water-snakes, some even basking on the rocks or slithering up onto the ledges of the cliffs.

Will you order your men to sound their war-horns, in the hope of scaring the water-snakes away (turn to **436**), or will you prepare to fight the slippery creatures (turn to **311**)?

## 418

Suddenly there is the roar of a flame and a searing glare before your eyes, and your nostrils fill with the smell of burning hair.

One of the bolder warriors has taken up a brand from the hearth-fire and struck you with it.

Roll one die and deduct this many *Endurance* points. Alternatively, pick a card and deduct that many *Endurance* points, unless if it is greater than 7 or a picture card, in which case deduct 6 *Endurance* points.

Now roll one die again (or pick a card); if the number rolled is odd (or the card is red), turn to **472**, but if the number rolled is even (or the card is black), turn to **19**.

## 419

Continue your battle with the Dragon, using the stats you already have recorded for the worm on your Adventure Sheet.

As soon as you have reduced its *Endurance* score by 12 points or more, or after another four Combat Rounds (whichever is sooner), turn to **299**.

If you wish, you may spend 1 *Hero Point* and turn to **299** straightaway.

## 420

"It lies north of here," says the slave, "where breakers beat at the headland like white-foam hammers. Below it, in the cliff-face, there is a certain cave, like a mouth. The entrance to the cairn is overgrown and almost hidden. In another age an ancient king hid his beloved riches there. Heaps of hoard-things fill an underground hall, the treasure of a long-dead race rusting and derelict."

Then it is your turn to speak:

| | |
|---|---|
| "Tell me more of the treasure-hoard's guardian." | Turn to **457**. |
| "Why did you take the cup?" | Turn to **438**. |

## 421

With the slithering things gone, and one of your warrior-band lying dead in the shallows, the water becomes calm again. You can see nothing beyond its mirror-black surface.

(Deduct 1 from your *Crew* score.)

Unanxious for your life, you double-check both your arms and armour, deciding which will be the best weapon with which to face Grendel's dam.

It is then that King Hrothgar's company arrives at the shores of that bitter pool, and Unferth – the same Unferth who goaded you regarding your swimming race with Breca – steps forward, his sword unbuckled and held out before him in its scabbard.

"Noble Beowulf," he says, his eyes cast down in contrition, "I was wrong to doubt you before, for you have proved yourself in battle with the fiend Grendel. And so now I offer you my sword, that you might use it to slay the monster's mother. It is called Hrunting, and it is a weapon both rare and ancient."

If you want to accept Unferth's offer, turn to **407**. If you politely decline, turn to **386**.

Still moving at speed, you reach the yawning mouth of the cave in the face of the cliff overlooking the tumultuous sea.

Do you want to use your momentum to throw yourself out of the cave and into the sea, to escape the Dragon (turn to **473**), or do you want to try to stop yourself before you pass the point of no return (turn to **346**)?

Stepping through the door, you enter a hall fit for a king, but a king long-dead. Carved stone pillars support its domed roof, and a noble throne, carved of dark wood and draped with a sheepskin, stands before another door on the other side of the chamber, as if its owner might return at any moment, and take his seat.

But this hall does not resound with harp-play or the joy of skald-told tales. This hall does not ring with the voices of thanes emboldened by mead, or the protests of the women who are the unhappy focus of their attentions. For this place was constructed by a race now death-rapt.

You are standing within a grand burial chamber. The king that commanded it to be built lies upon a stone bed, clad in tarnished armour, his ancient sword in hand. But there are two within his hall who do not sleep, a pair of thanes whose duty to their king remains long after death has made corpses of them.

Moving almost as one, in their deathly duty, they advance towards you, as one of them issues a challenge.

"Stand! Hwā dearr astyrian þæs cyninges ēcan slǣp on his reste?"

Turn to **8**.

You travel deeper and deeper into the earth, heading in a direction that you believe is taking you closer and closer to where the headland runs out and the cliffs meet the sea, until you find your way barred by a door. It is fashioned from stone and covered with ornate carvings, twisting serpents, and ancient runic script, which reads as follows:

> *With gold round my head, and steel in my hand,*
> *My word is law, throughout the whole land.*
> *I lead by example my warrior-band,*
> *'Gainst invaders and rebels I stand.*
> *If you know who I am, declare it now!*

The answer the riddle is one word. If you know the answer to the riddle, turn the letters of the word into numbers using the code A=1, B=2… Z=26, add them together, and turn to the section with the same number as the total.

If you are unable to work out the answer, or the section you turn to makes no sense when you read it – meaning you have got the answer wrong – turn to **167**.

You try to throw yourself out of the way as the chieftain turns his poisonous gaze upon you, but you are not quick enough.

As his baleful glare sweeps over you, you feel its strength-sapping effects immediately. The power drains from your muscles and you fall to the ground, suddenly feeling as weak and helpless as an infant.

As the giant reaches for you with a huge callused hand, in desperation you clutch at anything that might help you defend yourself. Finding a stone, with all the strength you can muster you hurl it at the giant. Odin must be guiding your hand, for the rock hits the chieftain in the eye, and he gives voice to another bellow, of pain this time, as your projectile blinds him.

Lose 4 *Endurance* points and 2 *Combat* points. If you are still alive, make a note that in the battle you are about to join your enemy has the initiative, and then turn to **394**.


### 426

The wyrm comes for you as you prepare to strike it dead with the wrathful war-tooth Gram. (In this battle, Fáfnir has the initiative.)

FÁFNIR                              COMBAT 8          ENDURANCE 12

If Fáfnir wins a Combat Round, roll one die (or pick a card) – if the number rolled is odd (or the card is red), you must lose an additional 1 *Endurance* point as the monster's toxic breath poisons you.

If you manage to slay the monster, turn to **490**. However, if Fáfnir kills you, turn to **464**.

If you wish you may spend 2 *Hero Points* to automatically win your battle with Fáfnir – turn to **490**.

## 427

In your dreams you see a shadow-shape skulking from the moorlands' misty fells. The march-haunter stalks the night with a clear purpose, his destination the witch-cursed, gold-panelled mead-hall of King Hrothgar…

\* \* \* \*

You are woken by a crashing knock upon the doors of Heorot that reverberates throughout the hall and sends showers of dust cascading from the rafters.

The banging comes again and this time the great iron-bound oak doors are sundered, and the splintered planks come crashing into the mead-hall.

"The monster!" Handscio, on sentry duty, cries. "Grendel is here!"

Turn to **159**.

## 428

"Noble king," you say, bowing your head and averting your eyes from the draugr's emaciated form, "I apologise for disturbing your rest, but I have come here to return that which was taken from you."

Taking out the Golden Goblet, you offer the gleaming treasure-cup to the draugr.

If you have Loki's Favour, turn to **460**.

If not, roll one die (or pick a card); if the number rolled is odd (or the card is red), turn to **178**, but if the number rolled is even (or the card is black), turn to **460**.

Alternatively, if you are able to, you may spend 1 *Hero Point* and turn to **460** anyway.

## 429

The monster howls in pain, desperately straining to break free and escape back to the darkness. But you are determined that he won't escape. After all, you have the upper hand now.

Reduce Grendel's *Combat* score by 2 points and continue your wrestling-match with the monster; you still have the initiative.

If you win two consecutive Combat Rounds or you are the first to win four Combat Rounds, turn to **469**. Alternatively, you may spend 1 *Hero Point* to turn to **469** straightaway.

If Grendel wins three consecutive Combat Rounds or five Combat Rounds in total first, turn to **254**.

## 430

The Trickster must be smiling upon you for suddenly, just when you thought Unferth had beaten you, the answer to the riddle comes to you, and you announce it with such a shout that it echoes from the gable-ends of the hall.

"Now try this, friend Unferth," you say, before issuing your own riddle-challenge.

> "I yearn to have what I had last night,
> Though it injures men and hinders each.
> The work of bees is my delight –
> Though it hurts heads, it elevates speech!
> What is it?"

Unferth stares at you blankly, with unfocused eyes. "I... I... I do not know," he concedes at last.

"The answer is mead!" you declare, taking a drinking-horn from the table. "Mead!" you say as you approach the defeated Unferth Kinslayer. "Mead!" you laugh as you empty the contents of the cup over his head.

Turn to **252**.

Snatching up the sleeping soldier, you tear at his body with your terrible fangs. Gnashing at his bone-joints and sucking at his veins, your jaws dripping with gore, you wolf down great gobbets of flesh until you have consumed everything, even the wretch's hands and feet.

Gain 4 *Endurance* points, record the kenning *Geat-Guard* on your Adventure Sheet, and then turn to **489**.

You lie! You are as untrustworthy as Loki the Trickster! To have got this far you must have acquired at least one of those things!

Lose 2 *Hero Points* and then return to **383** and make the correct choice.

You wake with a start, hearing your name being called...

At first light, flanked by your storm-warriors, you walk the length of the hall – the floor-timbers booming under your determined footfalls – for an audience with the King.

"Did you pass the night peacefully, my lord?" you ask the white-haired Hrothgar. "Such an urgent summons this morn has unsettled me. After all, as they say, when someone wakes you before cockcrow it is never to share good news."

"The Woe-Bringer has come again to Heorot!" Hrothgar wails. "And this time it has taken Aeshere! He was my closest counsellor; we stood shoulder to shoulder in battle."

"Who is this Woe-Bringer of whom you speak?" you ask the King, appalled. "Has Grendel returned? Was tearing off his arm not enough to kill that fell-fiend?"

Recalling the savage wound you dealt the Dane-killer, your gaze goes to the rafters of the hall, where Grendel's arm once hung, for it does not hang there now.

"No, it was *not* the hell-spawn Grendel. Another bloodthirsty monster entered my hall and committed murder within its walls. A terrible visitation, she sought vengeance for the killing you perpetrated here not two nights past."

"She?" you gasp in disbelief.

"That's right," confirms the King sorrowfully. "Revenge was her motive, but in furthering her son's blood-feud, she has gone too far!"

Hrothgar's roar of rage echoes from one gabled end of Heorot to the other.

"So the monster has a mother?" you snarl, feeling the King's anger and despair as deeply as you would your own.

"Aye, an outcast, a dweller in dread waters and cold currents, a begetter of evils, a sea-hag. But now the fiend's dam, in her savage grief, has stolen away the brightest and best of my company!"

"Tell me where this mother of monsters makes her home and I will put an end to her as I did her ogre-ish offspring!" you declare, ever the hero.

"I have heard it said, by subjects of mine – those that live beyond the palisade of my king's seat, in the fell-country – that they have seen such a pair of monstrous wayfarers, the monster and his dam, haunting the northern moors. Those country folk have known the exile from old by the name Grendel, and though they know his dam by sight as well, they know not who, or what, sired the monster."

"I do not need to know who sired the brute," you growl, "only where the monster's mother – Aeshere's abductor – can be found."

"The region in which she dwells lies beyond the bounds of my kingdom and is shunned by men. None claim sovereignty there. It is a region of wolf-fells, wind-picked moors, and treacherous fen-paths. The fiend's lair can be found where a torrent of water pours down dark cliffs and plunges into the earth, in an underground flood. There the mere lies, overhung with black, crag-rooted trees, hoary with frost.

"I have heard it said that an uncanny sight can be witnessed there at night, akin to a blazing fire in the water! And no man knows how far down its bottom lies. It is also said that a stag, pressed hard by hounds, will hide within that forest, but if the dogs persist, the deer will sooner die than risk swimming across those waters to save its life.

"The wind there can stir up wicked storms that whip the whirling waters higher, 'til they climb the clouds and clog the air, so that the skies seem to weep."

"Be not afeared, your majesty," you tell the King. "I will travel to this haunted place and rid you of your second demon, as I rid you of the first. I swear it!"

"Seek then, if you dare!" declares hoary-haired Hrothgar. "I shall reward the deed, as I did before, with gifts from my treasure-hoard. If you return again."

"We must all expect to leave our life on this earth," you tell the King, "just as we must strive to earn some measure of renown before death seeks us out. After all, daring is the thing for which a warrior will be remembered."

"The gods be praised that you sought our shore, brave Beowulf!" cries the King.

If you are to hunt down the monster Grendel's kinswoman, you will need to set out as quickly as possible, for fear of her escaping you or causing more harm elsewhere. But Hrothgar's talk of the gods makes you consider that it might be wise to ask them for help in your killing-quest, before setting out.

If you want to set out straightaway, without delay, turn to **468**. However, if you wish to pray at the shrine that stands outside the hall first, turn to **454**.

"Hall of the Wolf!" you proclaim.

Turn to **374**.

Despite their desperate efforts, and your exhorted urgings, there are simply not enough oar-pulling seafarers aboard the *Sea-Wolf* for the ship to out-race the rising squid-beast.

As the Kraken's slime-slick arms close about the timbers of the hull, you attack the curse-monster with your spiteful war-blade. (In this battle the Kraken has the initiative.)

KRAKEN                                    COMBAT 10        ENDURANCE 20

If you are still alive after 5 Combat Rounds, turn to **21**. Alternatively you may spend 1 *Hero Point* and turn to **21** straightaway.

The war-horns sing an eager battle-cry and at first it seems to have had the desired effect, as the water-snakes slither away before the bright phrases of the carynx. But it quickly becomes apparent that the noise has made the lake-dwellers angry.

Swerving up from the depths comes a sea-drake more monstrous than any you have so far seen – such a fish-finned serpent as will sally out to make havoc in the seas where ships sail – and makes for you position on the shore.

Will you command your warriors to attack the water-snakes, in the hope of gaining the upper hand against them (turn to **331**), or do you want to take up a bow and bring down the sea-drake before it reaches the lake-shore (turn to **458**)?

Holding your breath, you roll out of the path of the noxious cloud. Scrambling to your feet again, you prepare to fulfil your oath to the dvergr Reginn.

Turn to **426**.

"I hoped I might appease my master, by offering him such a gift, and so that my story might be believed," the slave says sheepishly.

"And in carrying the plated goblet to me, as a peace-offering, brought a curse down upon all our heads!" Wiglaf cries.

"What do you mean?" you ask, thoughts of another curse, spoken in a lightless cave, coming unbidden into your mind.

Turn to **457**.

Roll one die. This is the number of warriors you manage to hit with your improvised club. However, if you roll a 6 you have still only hit 5 warriors.

Make a note of how many more men you have taken out of the fight and then turn to **475**.

As you proceed along the new branch, you are forced to duck, as the roof gets lower and lower, until you emerge into a small cave and find yourself at a dead-end.

Lying on the sandy floor of the cave is the body of a warrior, or at least the remains of one. It is immediately clear that the dead man is not King Hrothgar's trusted friend, for this warrior still has his head, but on closer inspection it also becomes clear that this man has been dead a long time; his body has decomposed and is now little more than a skeleton clad in rotted garments and rusted armour.

As you are studying the warrior's remains, you realise that light levels in the cave are rising. Looking up you are startled to see a form coalescing like a luminous mist, in the cold air of the cave, as a sound like the keening of the wind reverberates from the glistening cave-walls enclosing you.

If you want to stay where you are and face whatever it is that is manifesting within the cave, turn to **304**. If you would rather quit this place before the visitation can fully form, you return to the intersection, and follow the other tunnel (turn to **280**).


### 441

In a high, clear voice, as sweet as honeyed mead, his fingers trembling over the strings of his harp, the skald sings of King Hrothgar's past triumphs and the heroic deeds of his youth.

"And behind the wall of water he found the entrance to the
monster's lair,
And delving deep, he sought it underground, to slay it and
seize its treasure-hoard."

But while you are listening to the poet sing you are neglecting your men. And so, taking your cup of mead, you join them at their banqueting table.

Turn to **406**.


### 442

Still running, you reach the gaping mouth of the cave in the cliff overlooking the tempestuous sea. But there is not time to slow down and stop yourself bursting out of the cave and plunging over the edge of the precipice.

As you pass the point of no return, you feel Wiglaf seize your arm in his firm grip, and he saves you from going over the edge, as he himself clings onto an outcrop at the cave's entrance. But before you can thank him, the Dragon catches up with you both.

As the serpent emerges from the hole in the cliff-face, your ring-mail catches on several bony protrusions on its scaled-skin, and you are dragged from Wiglaf's grasp.

The only thing you can do, to save yourself, is cling on as the fire-ravager takes to the air once more, with you now hanging from its side.

*Take a Combat test*, as you fight to hang on. If you pass the test, turn to **284**, but if you fail the test, you lose your grip on the worm's scaly hide as the links of your war-mail tear free – turn to **473**.

If you want, you may spend 1 *Hero Point* rather than have to take the test at all, and turn to **284** straightaway.

### 443

Your mounting anger lending your muscles strength, you hurl Grendel's mother to the ground.

But as she scrambles to her feet again, she draws a knife, broad and burnished.

Turn to **359**.

### 444

When the flame of the clouds rises in the sky the following dawn, the outrage you have committed against King Hrothgar's company is openly seen by all, the night's table-laughter having become the morning's lamentations.

Having a taste now for man-flesh, you return the next night, intent on bringing new horrors to the Danes' door, your heart burning with a deep and dark desire to maim, murder, and man-slaughter.

But as you approach high-antlered Heorot, you do not hear sounds of mirth and merriment coming from within the stockade, nor the snores of soundly sleeping soldiers, but the jangle of mail-harness and the ring of the whetstone on sharpened steel.

Do you want to approach the stockade that surrounds Hrothgar's hall by the main gates (turn to **478**), or would you prefer to find another way inside (turn to **459**)?

### 445

You throw yourself out of the way as the giant's baleful gaze sweeps over the spot where you had been standing, until only a moment ago.

Picking up a stone from the gravel bed of the river, you hurl it at the giant. Odin must be guiding your hand, for the rock hits the chieftain in the eye, and he gives voice to another bellow, of pain this time, as your projectile blinds him.

Make a note that in the battle you are about to join, you have the initiative, and then turn to **394**.

First it is the rattle of ring-mail, then the clatter of swords, and finally two figures step into the pool of light cast by the torch held high in your hand.

They are clad in warriors' garb, and come armed with blood-biters, ready to fight, but their long hair is lank, their skin grey, and where their eyes should be are empty pits of darkness.

You have run across two more of the barrow-king's unsleeping shieldsmen, patrolling his earthen hall, and have no choice but to defend yourself against the un-dead warriors. (In this battle, the draugr have the initiative, and you must fight them both at the same time.)

|  | COMBAT | ENDURANCE |
|---|---|---|
| First DRAUGR WARRIOR | 8 | 7 |
| Second DRAUGR WARRIOR | 7 | 7 |

If you wish, you may spend 2 *Hero Points* to automatically win this battle (turn to **482**).

If not, conduct the battle as normal and, if you defeat both your opponents, only then turn to **482**.

You wait and wait, as the rush-lamps slowly dim and your men try to get some rest, after the exertions of the day.

And then, when the only light within the hall comes from the slumbering coals in the fire-pit of Hrothgar's hearth, you are shaken alert by a crashing knock upon the doors that reverberates throughout the hall and sends dust-showers cascading from the rafters.

The banging comes again and this time the great iron-bound oak doors give way at the monster's unkind caresses, and the splintered planks come crashing halfway down the hall.

"The monster!" the sentry Handscio cries. "Grendel is here!"

Turn to **159**.

Blood pours from the wound in the wyrm's underbelly, soaking your hair, your clothes and your skin. And there is so much of it! It is a red tide that rapidly fills the pit with a crimson flood. However, because you dug a series of ditches rather than a simple pit, enough of the vile fluid runs off into the other trenches that you don't drown in the wyrm's blood.

Fáfnir thrashes its long neck and tail in its death-throes, gouging the earth and tearing up plants in its thrashing frenzy, roaring in pain at the mortal wound you have dealt it.

Fighting the blood-muddied sides of the pit to clamber out again, with your wrathful war-tooth in hand, you prepare to finish the beast. (In this battle you have the initiative.)

FÁFNIR                    COMBAT 6        ENDURANCE 6

If Fáfnir wins a Combat Round, roll one die (or pick a card) – if the number rolled is odd (or the card is red), you must lose an additional 1 *Endurance* point as the monster's toxic breath poisons you.

If you slay the monster, turn to **490**. However, if Fáfnir kills you, turn to **464**.

If you wish you may spend 1 *Hero Point* to automatically win your battle with Fáfnir – turn to **490**.

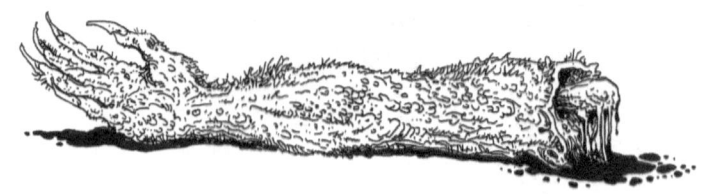

Grendel comes for you, hurling your men out of the way to get to you, reaching for you with a spite-filled fist. But you swiftly lay hold of him and the two of you grapple. (In this hand-to-hand contest of strength, Grendel has the initiative.)

GRENDEL                         COMBAT 10         ENDURANCE 12

Conduct the wrestling-match as you would any other battle, but if you or the monster win a Combat Round do not deduct any *Endurance* points from the loser of that Combat Round; instead, keep a track of how many Combat Rounds each of you wins.

If you win three consecutive Combat Rounds or you are the first to win five Combat Rounds in total, turn to **469**. Alternatively, you may spend 1 *Hero Point* and turn to **469** immediately.

If Grendel is the first to win three consecutive Combat Rounds or five Combat Rounds, turn to **254**.

Beowulf, the hero of the Storm-folk of Geatland, is dead, by your savage hand. His war-band flees in terror as you tear his body limb from limb, painting the walls of Heorot red with his wound-sweat.

None can best you in battle. You rule within the Hall of the Stag now, the night your realm, the fells your kingdom, and none shall ever challenge you again.

The darkness has a champion, one whose name will be spoken of in legend for a thousand generations to come, that of Grendel Grimslayer!

# THE END

## 451

You stand shoulder-to-shoulder with your men as you prepare to face the thrashing water-snakes, and find yourself facing one of the largest specimens. (In this battle, the water-snake has the initiative.)

WATER-SNAKE                    COMBAT 6        ENDURANCE 7

If you want to ensure that you win this fight, you may spend 1 *Hero Point* and turn to **421** straightaway.

If not, conduct the battle as normal and, if you win, then turn to **421**.

## 452

Dodging the falling blocks of masonry, you sprint for the cave mouth that is the Dragon's way in and out of the barrow-hoard chamber. But as you run, you hear the sucking, gale-wind roar of the worm drawing in a great breath, only for it to exhale again a moment later, sending a fearsome fire-blast chasing after you.

If you have Freya's Favour, turn to **381**.

If not, *Take an Endurance test*. If you pass the test, turn to **381**, but if you fail the test, turn to **408**.

Alternatively, if you want to ensure that fatigue does not slow your pace, you may deduct 1 *Hero Point* and turn to **381** anyway.

## 453

"It means 'Hall of the Stag', you tell the watchman. "Now lead us there so we might rid King Hrothgar of his curse."

"You speak of the curse," the Coast Warden replies, not moving the spear still pointing at your heart, "but do you know for how long the troll-born bone-grinder has tormented us?"

If you do know the answer, turn to the section that has the same number as the number of years Grendel has vexed the Danes.

If you do not know the answer, or the section you turn to makes no sense, turn to **313** instead.

## 454

It seems likely to you that the reason Heorot is in such turmoil is because the god Loki is toying with Hrothgar and the Spear-Danes.

Within the shrine stands a huge wooden effigy of the god, with deep-carved eyes and a curling moustache that follows the outline of a smiling mouth. And so you pray to Loki, the Trickster, the Magician, beseeching him to help rather than hinder you in your quest.

Record Loki's Favour on your Adventure Sheet, if you do not already have it written down, and turn to **468**.

## 455

"Very well, friend Unferth," you declare with good cheer, "I accept your challenge."

"Then here is my first!" Unferth says, clearing his throat.

> "I'll fight with the wind, and war with the wave,
> But if stones hold me firm, the ship I'll save.
> What am I?"

The answer to Unferth's riddle is a single simple noun. If you know the answer, turn the letters of the word into numbers using the code A=1, B=2… Z=26, add them together, double the total, and turn to the section with the same number as this final total.

If you cannot solve the riddle, or the section you turn to makes no sense when you read it, turn to **487**.

## 456

Blood-smoke fills the air around you and, with a terrible roar, its beating wings parting the spark-shot cloud, the Dragon is there before you once more, jaws yawning wide as it gives voice to its fiery-roar.

If you have The Lord's Favour, turn to **491**. If not, turn to **235**.

## 457

"A dragon, such as in the legends of old, sleeps within the barrow, its coiled body encircling the hoard," whimpers the slave.

"Or at least it did!" Wiglaf wails. "The guardian might have been caught sleeping by this cunning cup-thief, but it sleeps no longer, and in fury at discovering its loss has roused itself and left the barrow, seeking revenge.

"Fire has been seen to the north, a forest burnt to ash by its furious flame-rage. The Dragon has woken from its sleep of centuries and is heading this way, seeking the wretch who stole from its hoard!"

The situation is dire indeed! Never have your people needed their strong-defender more than now!

Will you order your men to move against the Ravager without delay (turn to **476**), or will you wait within your hall and prepare for the Dragon's coming (turn to **495**)?

One of your storm-warriors hands you his bow and, nocking a swift dart to the string, you draw it back, the supple wood groaning as you do so.

If you want to make sure that your arrow finds its mark, deduct 1 *Hero Point* and turn to **477**.

If you do not want to do this, or you do not have any *Hero Points* left to spend, *Take a Combat test*; if you pass the test, turn to **477**, but if you fail the test, turn to **291**.

Behind the high staked ring-fence you find a stinking culvert – little more than a muddy channel, ripe with the reek of ale-waste and ordure – that has washed a channel under the stockade, and it is via this open sewer that you gain entry to King Hrothgar's demesne unseen.

Add the kenning *Sewer-Stink* to your Adventure Sheet and then turn to **56**.

Slowly, the King lowers his weapon but the furious lights still blaze in the sockets of his mouldering skull.

"You invade my sanctuary, making all manner of claims and telling me what you think I want to hear, but your deeds speak louder than your words."

The draugr indicates his slain sentries.

"You cut down my noble thanes, as if they were stalks of wheat, and yet you do not even offer me blood-geld in recompense, in an attempt to make amends!"

If you have a Purse of Ancient Coins, you will know how many coins the purse contains; turn to that section now.

If you do not have such a purse, or you do not want to give the coins to the King, turn to **178**.

### 461

With mounting anger, you try to hurl the ogress to the ground. But then her own ruthless hands reach out for you, and you stumble in your weariness, falling to the ground.

She draws her own knife now – broad and burnished – with which she intends to avenge the death of her only son.

If you are wearing the Silver Corselet, turn to **486**. If not, turn to **499**.

### 462

At your behest, the men start to sing: bawdy songs of the womenfolk they have ravaged on their raiding-jaunts across the sea; songs passed down by the poets, from skald to skald, of monsters slain and heroes feted; songs that raise their spirits and bolster their courage as surely as Hrothgar's free-flowing mead.

(Add 1 point to your *Combat* score.)

Your chanting warriors are suddenly silenced by a terrible banging upon the doors of Heorot that is loud enough to wake the dead.

It comes again. This time, the great iron-bound oak doors give way at the monster's unkind caresses, and the splintered planks come crashing into the hall.

"The monster!" the sentry Handscio cries. "Grendel is here!"

And then Grendel, the devourer of men bursts into the hall.

The monster is truly terrible to behold – with wyrm-scales, bear-claws, and a beast's hide, its hulking form long-limbed, sinew-knotted and corded all about with muscle – but you are Geats and not so easily frightened.

It will take more than a moorland-monster like Grendel to make your blood run cold.

Turn to **209**.

The Dragon uncoils from about the treasure-mound, ready to drive you from the usurped hoard-hall.

It is a terrible creature – all wings, and fangs and tearing talons – but you are King Beowulf – the Bee-Wolf, the Bear, the Berserker – and your vengeful fury will not be denied.

Taking up your sword you defend yourself against the serpent-worm. (In this battle, the Dragon has the initiative.)

DRAGON                    COMBAT 10      ENDURANCE 50

If you reduce the Dragon's *Endurance* score to 42 points or fewer, or after 4 Combat Rounds (whichever is sooner), turn to **403**.

Alternatively, you may spend 1 *Hero Point* and turn to **403** straightaway.

## 464

Despite coming to this desolate place to slay the wyrm, it is Fáfnir that has slain you. You end your days left in a bloody pit, to be devoured at a time of the wyrm's choosing…

Turn to **479**.

## 465

Three of the giants lie dead now, at your hand. As the effects of the druid's fearful spell pass, the chieftain of the jotunn-kin bears down on you, giving voice to a dreadful bull-bellow and attempting to fix you with his baleful stare.

A strip of grubby sail-cloth bound around his head covers his left eye, but as he stomps towards you, he lifts this covering and you see the turf wither and blacken, where his baleful gaze strikes.

As the chief's gaze falls upon your men they stumble and fall, sapped of strength. And then the giant turns its withering wyrd-power in your direction.

*Take an Agility test.* If you pass the test, turn to **445**, but if you fail the test, turn to **425**. Alternatively, you may spend 1 *Hero Point* to avoid having to take the test at all, and turn to **445** immediately.

## 466

First it is the rattle of ring-mail, then the clatter of swords, and then two figures step into the pool of light cast by the torch held high in your hand.

They are clad in warriors' garb, and come armed with blood-biters, ready to fight, but their long hair is lank, their skin grey, and where their eyes should be are empty pits of darkness.

You have run across two more of the barrow-king's unsleeping shieldsmen, patrolling his earthen hall, and have no choice but to defend yourself against the un-dead warriors. As Wiglaf engages the first of them, desirous to prove to you what a great hero he could be, you tackle the second of the draugr. (In this battle, the draugr warrior has the initiative.)

DRAUGR WARRIOR          COMBAT 7          ENDURANCE 7

If you wish, you may spend 1 *Hero Point* to automatically win this battle (turn to **482**).

If not, conduct the battle as normal and, if you defeat your opponent, only then turn to **482**.

### 467

If you have Loki's Favour or Njord's Favour recorded on your Adventure Sheet, turn to **36**.

If you have neither of these favours, roll one die (or pick a card); if the number rolled is odd (or the card is red), turn to **343**, but if the number rolled is even (or the card is black), turn to **36**.

Alternatively, if you are able to, you may spend 1 *Hero Point* and turn to **36** no matter what.

### 468

Inspired by your heroic speech (gain 1 *Hero Point*), Hrothgar, the hero-patriarch, prepares to ride out with his retinue after you. A steed with braided mane is bridled for the King, while a troop of shield-bearers prepares to march out beside him.

But you cannot wait for the King; you must away.

Having been supplied with 3 Meals' worth of provisions by the King's cooks, you set off.

If you have the kenning *Dark-Mere* written on your Adventure Sheet, turn to **488**. If not, turn to **378**.

You manage to get a grip on Grendel's arm and strain with all your might, tightening your hold until the monster's fingers snap like twigs. The brute-beast cries out in agony even as it tries to break free of your clutches, so that the Danes – who must surely be waiting outside the hall now, drawn by the sounds of battle within – hear Grendel's grisly cry for mercy.

*Take an Endurance test*. If you pass the test, turn to **498**, but if you fail the test, turn to **484**. Alternatively, you may spend 1 *Hero Point* and automatically turn to **498**.

You and your fellow Geats are made welcome within Heorot.

Mighty in your ring-meshed hauberk, your silver helm still upon your head, you stand tall before Hrothgar and his karls, your men arrayed in a thick throng behind you.

"So tell us, Beowulf," says King Hrothgar, "what brings you across the whale-road to our shores?"

"I have come to serve you, noble lord," you begin, "for the skalds sing of King Hrothgar's Curse from the ice-locked north to the rain-lashed south, and from the lands of the Frisians in the west to the untamed forests of the Rus to the east."

At your mention of his curse, a shadow passes over the old king's face.

"Travellers speak of great Heorot standing silent, as soon as the night's shadow falls. All Geats have heard of your plight, how the monster Grendel – the flesh-grinder – prowls this pillared hall and preys upon your people, eating of their flesh and drinking of their blood."

A murmur passes among the gathered thanes.

"I am Beowulf Giant-killer, Beowulf the Serpent-slayer, and I am here to test my mettle against this fear of the fells, this monster of the moors, this Grendel! I will rid you of your troll-born demon and lift the curse that lies upon Heorot."

An expectant hush falls over the hall and all assembled within, and then Hrothgar speaks.

"The gods have blessed us in sending you to our shores, friend Beowulf, and if you can indeed rid us of our tormentor, you shall be richly rewarded for this kindness. My company is diminished, and my ranks of warriors too, wyrd-doomed to fall into the clutches of that ogre Grendel. And it pains me to tell you that many war-bright champions have made the same promise as you have this day, when deep in their cups. Emboldened by ale they have waited in this wassailing-place, with weapons bone-sharp, ready to meet the horror Grendel with the terror of their own blades. But always it was the same; when morning came their blood painted the benches, walls and floor of Heorot, making a slaughterhouse of my shining hall.

"But maybe this time it will be different. Come, Beowulf, we shall hold a feast in your honour, and hope that the fare of this hero's banquet does not coldly furnish forth your funeral feast."

Turn to **492**.

You stand shoulder-to-shoulder with your men as you prepare to deal with these dwellers of the depths. Naturally, you seek out the largest specimen, so that your mind's-worth might grow as bards recount the tale of your battle with the water-snakes in years to come. (In this battle, you have the initiative.)

WATER-SNAKE                    COMBAT 6          ENDURANCE 7

If you want to ensure that you win this fight, you may spend 1 *Hero Point* and turn to **421** straightaway. If not, conduct the battle as normal and, if you win, then turn to **421**.


## 472

The brand-bearer's attack has set fire to the thick fur that covers your body.

Record the kenning *Life-Harm* on your Adventure Sheet and then turn to **19**.


## 473

You drop like a stone, but rather than landing in the churning, storm-tossed waves, you hit the ragged rocks that lie at the foot of the breaker-beaten cliffs. There is no escaping death this time, not even for a hero such as you.

Your adventure is over.

# THE END

You travel deeper and deeper into the earth, heading in a direction that you believe is taking you closer and closer to where the headland runs out and the cliffs meet the sea, until you find your way barred by a door. It is fashioned from stone and covered with ornate carvings, twisting serpents, and ancient runic script, which appears as follow:

ᚹᛁᛏᚺ ᚷᛟᛟᛞ ᚱᛟᚢᚾᛞ ᛗᛁ ᛞᛖᚪᛞ ᚻᚾᛞ ᛋᛏᛖᛖᛚ ᛁᛋ ᛗᛁ ᚻᚾᛞ

ᛗᛁ ᚹᛟᚱᛞ ᛁᛋ ᛚᚪᚹ ᛏᚺᚱᛟᚢᚷᚺᛟᚢᛏ ᛏᚺᛖ ᚹᚾᛟᛚᛖ ᛚᚪᚾᛞ

ᛁ ᛚᛖᚪᛞ ᛒᛁ ᛗᛒᚪᛗᛈᛚᛖ ᛗᛁ ᚹᚪᚱᚱᛁᛟᚱ ᛒᚪᚾᛞ

ᚠᚷᚻᛁᛋᛏ ᛁᚾᚡᚪᛞᛖᚱᛋ ᚻᚾᛞ ᚱᛗᛒᛖᛚᛋ ᛁ ᛋᛏᚪᚾᛞ

ᛁᚠ ᛃᛟᚢ ᚲᚾᛟᚹ ᚹᚾᛟ ᛁ ᚪᛗ ᛞᛟᛗᚲᚪᚱᛗ ᛁᛏ ᚾᛟᚹ

It is a riddle, the answer to which is one word. If you know the answer to the riddle, turn the letters of the word into numbers using the code A=1, B=2… Z=26, add them together, and turn to the section with the same number as the total.

If you are unable to work out the answer, or the section you turn to makes no sense when you read it – meaning you have got the answer wrong – turn to **167**.

## 475

The remaining men run at you then with swords drawn. You meet their attack with sweeping slashes of your long claws.

*Take a Combat test.* If you pass the test, turn to **350**, but if you fail the test, turn to **323**.

## 476

You set out with your entourage, a dozen of your finest warriors, to engage the flame-spewer before it can ever reach your royal seat.

Mounted upon your barded war-steeds, you ride hard into the encroaching darkness, into the icy teeth of the bitter wind. And then you see the winged monster as it swims through the gloom, enfolded in flame, as it flies across the sky, far out of reach of your bows and good intentions.

As your horses gallop along the northern road, the Dragon descends upon your hall. There is nothing you can do but watch, horror writ large upon your face and a rage that burns as hot as the Dragon's breath within your heart, as the evil creature douses your hall and the houses of your karls with flame, razing them to the ground.

When all is aflame – from your high-gabled hall to the proud stockade and settlement that surrounds it – the shimmering-scaled monster flies back to its barrow-cave lair, on wings underlit by the fires left in its wake.

Turn to **175**.

## 477

The arrow flies straight and true, and the iron tip of the dart lodges in the wave-thrasher's throat, breaking its life's-thread.

The sea-drake continues to churn through the water, making it to the shallows before death takes it at last. Your men splash into the lake and, using their barbed boar-spears, drag the creature up to the cliff-top.

You gaze with wonder upon this strange lurker of the waves – with its bloated body, oar-like fins and eel-like head atop a neck as long as a longship's mast – and wonder how many heroes it has devoured in its life, and what treasures might lie within its belly.

If you want to order your men to open it up and see what lies within, turn to **496**. If you would prefer not to rummage through the stinking guts of the lake-monster, turn to **354**.


### 478

After the slaughter you committed against their kin the previous night, the Danes are now wise to your evil ways, mirth-killer, and have set sentries at the gate. Where before Hrothgar's thanes were complacent, now they are concerned. Where once they were slow to react, now they are quick to arms. And they are waiting for you. (In this battle, the sentries have the initiative.)

SENTRIES                    COMBAT 8        ENDURANCE 10

If you slay the sentries, turn to **56**.


### 479

"And so ends the Saga of Sigurd, Last of the Völsungs," announces the skald with one final flourish, rippling his harp strings.

Restore your *Agility*, *Combat* and *Endurance* scores to the levels they were before the poet started his recitation, and then turn to **89**.

## 480

The passageway you are following winds down through the bedrock of the fells until it opens out into a large cavern. You are standing at the edge of a limpid pool and it appears that, if you are going to proceed any further, you are going to have to enter its icy waters. You certainly can't see any sign of the monsters having made their home in this cave.

If you have the Helruna's Curse recorded on your Adventure Sheet, turn to **493**. If not, turn to **296**.

## 481

"Thank you, Unferth, my ale-emboldened friend, for reminding me of that particular incident, for it makes a greater story than that of giants and water-demons combined," you say, also rising to your feet.

"I too have heard that Breca brags he bested me in that race, but I know that it was I who had the greater sea-strength that day, for I endured a struggle beneath the waves that would have seen the end of him. And I will tell you of it now."

Make a note of your current *Agility*, *Combat* and *Endurance* scores and then turn to **251**.

## 482

The un-dead now truly dead, you are considering how best to proceed through the barrow-king's domain when you think you see something else moving in the gloom ahead of you.

Turn to **497**.

The Dragon uncoils from about the treasure-mound, ready to drive you from the usurped hoard-hall.

It is a terrible creature – all wings, and fangs and tearing talons – but you are King Beowulf – the Bee-Wolf, the Bear, the Berserker – and your vengeful fury will not be denied.

Taking up your sword, you defend yourself against the serpent-worm. (In this battle, the Dragon has the initiative.)

DRAGON                    COMBAT 10        ENDURANCE 50

Wiglaf will aid you in battling the Dragon. Each Combat Round you will have two attacks rather than just one; if you win either you will injure the Dragon, but if you win both, you do double damage for that Combat Round. However, the Dragon is focusing its attacks against you, so if it wins a Combat Round, you will be the one who comes to harm.

If you reduce the Dragon's *Endurance* score to 42 points or fewer, or after 4 Combat Rounds (whichever is sooner), turn to **403**.

Alternatively, you may spend 1 *Hero Point* and turn to **403** straightaway.

Spurred by the pain, Grendel claws at you with his free arm, raking your flesh with his cruel claws. You involuntarily loosen your grip on his scaly limb, enabling the monster to free himself from your crushing hold entirely.

Turn to **254**.

You manage to resist the druid's pernicious charm, but Gunnar and the others fighting by your side do not. You can see them quailing and quaking in terror, even retreating before the giant's advance, as a pall of fear falls over them.

There is only one way to shatter the charm, and that is to slay the charm-weaver. With a battle-cry, you charge at the druid. (In this battle, you have the initiative.)

DAGDA THE DRUID          COMBAT 7          ENDURANCE 10

After two Combat Rounds another ogre hurries to the soothsayer's defence. From the third Combat Round onwards you must fight both giants at the same time, that is, until one of them is defeated.

CROM THE CROOKED          COMBAT 8          ENDURANCE 11

If you somehow manage to defeat both the giants, turn to **465**, but if you lose the battle, turn to **79**.


### 486

Spread across your back, the corselet shields you from harm, barring entry to the sea-hag's notched knife by either point or edge. Edgetheow's son would have ended his venture deep underground were it not for that war-shirt of silvered steel.

Turn to **359**.


### 487

For the life of you, you cannot think of an answer to Unferth's riddle.

If you have Loki's Favour, turn to **430**. If not, turn to **334**.


### 488

You know of the lake where Grendel's dam dwells, beneath its black waters, having been there already, after you pursued the mortally injured monster to that accursed spot. You will have no trouble finding it again.

If you have the kenning *Shadow-Fast* written on your Adventure Sheet, turn to **414**. If not, turn to **398**.

The champion comes for you then, as his followers chant his name: "Beowulf! Beowulf! Beowulf!"

But, to your surprise, the young warrior ducks beneath your sweeping talons and seizes hold of your arm. You have never encountered one of the human race as strong as he and so commence your struggle to free yourself from his clutches. (In this battle, Beowulf has the initiative.)

BEOWULF                 COMBAT 10      ENDURANCE 10

Conduct the wrestling-match as you would any other battle, but if you or Beowulf win a Combat Round do not deduct any *Endurance* points from the loser. Instead, keep a track of how many Combat Rounds each of you wins.

If you win two consecutive Combat Rounds or you are the first to win four Combat Rounds, turn to **290**.

If Beowulf is the first to win two consecutive Combat Rounds or four Combat Rounds in total, turn to **336**.

Feeling its life slipping away, with its last breath, the wyrm suddenly gasps, "You have bested me, warrior, and for releasing me from my self-imposed curse, I reward you. Ride away from this place and leave my treasure-hoard untouched, for if you take even one piece from the hoard a great doom will find you." With that, the mighty wyrm dies.

Pulling Gram from the wyrm's body, you wipe the bloody blade on the withered grass of the heath. As you are returning the sword to its sheathe, Reginn the dwarf rides up and gazes at the monster's corpse with greedy eyes.

"Since it was I who forged the blade that killed the wyrm," he says, hungrily, "might I have the honour of eating its heart?"

The dvergr is right – without his help, and Gram in your hand, you doubt you could have slain Fáfnir.

"It would be *my* honour," you tell the dwarf, "and I will even cook it for you."

And so you prepare a fire and set the wyrm's heart on a spit over it, to roast. In time you put a finger to the heart to see if it is cooked but burn yourself. Without thinking, you stick your finger in your mouth, to cool the burn, and in doing so taste the monster's blood.

Suddenly, hearing the twitter of voices, you turn to see four birds hopping about on the heath, brave now that the beast is dead. But, unbelievably, you can understand what the birds are saying.

"You cannot trust the dwarf," says one of them, clearly addressing you.

"He plans to eat the heart to gain wisdom and the power of prophecy," twitters another.

"Then he will murder you and steal Fáfnir's treasure," chirrups a third.

"Better you should eat the heart yourself and do away with your treacherous companion," whistles the fourth.

You look across the fire at Reginn and see the truth of what the birds have told you in his eyes.

So, taking the wrathful blade Gram from its scabbard once more, you strike the dwarf's head from his shoulders before eating the wyrm's heart yourself.

Leaving the bodies of Reginn and Fáfnir behind, you mount your horse and ride to the wyrm's lair, where you find a king's ransom in gold and jewels. Ignoring the wyrm's talk of curses, you load everything – every last coin and gem – onto your horse, and head for home.

Gain 3 *Hero Points*, make a note of the fact that four birds helped save your life on your Adventure Sheet, and then turn to **479**.

As you face the worm again, you feel of the power of the Lord fill you.

For the rest of the duration of your battle with the Dragon, you may add 1 point when calculating your *Combat Rating*.

Now turn to **235**.

And so the mead-hall is swept, fresh rushes are laid upon the floor, while a hero's feast is prepared. Once again the Hall of the Stag will ring to the rafters with music and merry-making.

A bench is cleared for your company of Geats, the food is served, the mead is poured, and the song of the skald is heard in Heorot once more, while you make your way among your men.

If you want to take a moment to listen to the skald, turn to **441**. If you would prefer to sit and eat with your men, turn to **406**.

A high-pitched squeaking and the agitated fluttering of wings has you looking to the ceiling. Skin-winged and black-furred, the bats fly down from where they have been roosting among the stalactites hanging from the vaulted roof of the cave. But you are blocking their way out.

Fight the bats as if they were one creature, and in this battle it is the bats that have the initiative.

COLONY OF BATS          COMBAT 6          ENDURANCE 8

If you fend off the Bats, or after four Combat Rounds, whichever is sooner, turn to **404**.

If you would prefer not to have to conduct the battle with the bats, you may spend 1 *Hero Point* and automatically turn to **404** instead.

As you fight to free yourself, suddenly, with a horrible sucking ripping sound, your shoulder tears open, as flesh and bone fail you. Accompanied by the sound of sinews snapping and bone-locks bursting, in a welter of black blood, your arm is ripped from its socket!

The scream that bursts from you then stops the blood of all who hear it – even the berserker known as Beowulf – and in that moment of cruel realisation, you flee from the hall, leaving your still-twitching limb in the warrior's grisly grasp.

Desperate and death-sick, clutching at the wound with your remaining claw, and howling like a wolf in your anguish, you return to the fens and the fells, and the lake-lair you share with your dam. Back in the cave beneath the lake, you lie down to die, knowing that your time has come, your life ended by Beowulf Beastslayer…

Your adventure is over.

# THE END

**495**

While your warriors ready their weapons, you set your liege weapon-smith to work. But what do you want him to do?

Sharpen your sword?                                       Turn to **321**.

Fashion you a new shield?                                  Turn to **344**.

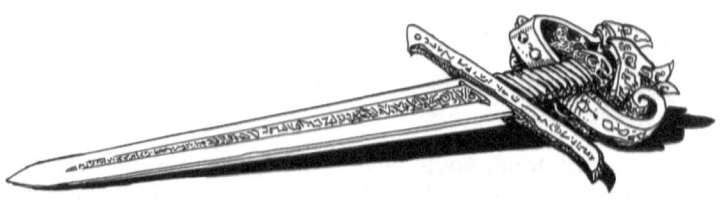

Taking their blades to the beast, your Geats slice open its belly. A stinking slurry of half-digested fish and foul blood gushes out onto the rocks. The stench is truly terrible.

(For the duration of the next battle you fight, you must reduce your *Combat Rating* by 1 point, as you are near overcome by the nauseating stench of the dead drake's stomach contents.)

However, amidst the stomach-gruel you see the glint of metal. Daring to peer closer, you see that it is a talisman in the form of a fish. Plucking it from the mess you wash it in the lake and see that the talisman hangs from a silver chain.

If you want to put on the Fish Talisman, add it to your Adventure Sheet, and then turn to **354**.

It was nothing, merely a trick of the light, a false threat conjured by the lambent flame of your torch.

Since entering the barrow, you will have acquired one or more kennings. If you only have the kenning *Battle-Hood* written down, turn to **123**. If you only have the kenning *Earth-Maw* written down, turn to **69**. If you have both *Battle-Hood* and *Earth-Maw* recorded on your Adventure Sheet, turn to **86**.

You have the monster pinioned now and will not let go. You twist and twist until a rip appears in the unnatural hide of the ogre, as flesh and bone fail him. A dire wound opens upon his shoulder, accompanied by the dreadful sound of tendons snapping and bone-locks bursting.

In your berserker fury, with your dread bear-strength you rip the demon's arm from its socket!

The scream that bursts from the monster turns the blood flowing through the veins of every warrior within the hall to pack-ice.

You tumble backwards, as Grendel's twitching limb comes away from the rest of his body, giving the monster the opportunity he needs to flee Heorot, desperate and death-sick, clutching at what must surely be a mortal wound, with his other bloodied paw, and howling like a wolf in his anguish.

The green-flamed rush-lamps are extinguished as he rushes out of the hall.

(Gain 2 *Hero Points* for defeating the monster.)

You have savagely wounded Grendel, but the fen-lurker was still alive when he fled the hall.

Do you want to set off in pursuit of the monster (turn to **194**), or will you stay where you are and recover your strength, certain that if the monster is not dead yet, then it will be soon (turn to **214**)?


### 499

The hag's blade sinks between your ribs, and your life-blood, that vital force that animates all living things, starts to pour out from the wound.

Lose 3 *Endurance* points and, if you are still alive, turn to **359**.


### 500

Thanks to the healing magic of the dead king's gift, and your own heroic constitution, you not only fight the effects of the Dragon's fiery venom, but the savage wounds the serpent dealt you begin to knit together, your body healing itself from what many would have considered a lethal wound.

Rallying and taking command of your wits once more, your grip on your sword like steel again, you thrust the blade into the Dragon's skull. The Ravager opens its mouth as it roars its pain, releasing you, even as the spark of life is driven from it.

And so you slay the Dragon.

This great accomplishment is not to be the last victory in a long life of daring deeds, for the wound the fire-drake inflicted upon you has, miraculously, already healed.

You have guarded the Geats for half a century, and in all that time not a single ruler of all the neighbouring nations has dared affront you with his allies in war. Who knows what else you might achieve in a life already long-lived, especially when measured against that of other heroes? For now it is time to forge your legend anew.

In time, your body will inevitably be relinquished to the flames of the funeral-pyre, and then there will be much mourning and misery among the people of your kingdom. But your name shall live on, eventually passing into legend, just as the mighty deeds you have performed in life become myths, part of a tale that will be told a thousand thousand times for a thousand years and more. The saga of Beowulf Beastslayer!

# THE END

# Grendel Grimslayer

And in those days of yore, the clan-king Hrothgar Dane-Father raised a hall, the like of which had never been seen under heaven, and named it Heorot.

But as you prowl the fens and fells of the hinterlands that gnaw at the borders of Hrothgar's kingdom, you are forced to endure the sounds of merriment and amusement that reach your wolf-sharp hearing, even across so many leagues, and it is as poison to you.

The music of the skald's harp is as a saw-blade grating against your bones, the clear song of the poet a bat-shriek in your ears. For you are a descendant of that race of monsters born from the darkness, hidden from the light of the sun, as from the light of knowledge and civilisation.

For you are the hag-born fen-fiend, the dweller in darkness, Grendel Grimslayer.

(Create a new character, just as you would normally.)

You crouch within your cave, the lake-lair where you lurk with your hag-mother the ogress, and as the men of Hrothgar's company go about their daily lives, heedless of the horrors that await them, you encompass evil, plotting their downfall and the destruction of the mead-hall Heorot.

At last you emerge from your fen-fell fastness and leave your haunt, the border-marches, crossing over into the lands of men. With the coming of night, you arrive at the great-house of the Spear-Danes, silence having fallen over the mead-hall.

But you have a purpose, and the peace of the night will not deter you from your task.

With the strength that is in your mighty arms, you break open the doors of the hall and burst inside.

Roll one die (or pick a card); if the number rolled is odd (or the card is red), turn to **138**, but if the number rolled is even (or the card is black), turn to **25**.

# THE RIDDLE OF THE RUNES

| ᚠ | ᛒ | ᚲ | ᛥ | ᛗ |
|---|---|---|---|---|
| A | B | C | D | E |

| ᚤ | ᚷ | ᚺ | ᛁ | ᛋ |
|---|---|---|---|---|
| F | G | H | I | J |

| ᚲ | ᚱ | ᛗ | ᛊ | ᛟ |
|---|---|---|---|---|
| K | L | M | N | O |

| ᛈ | ◇ | ᚱ | ᛋ | ↑ |
|---|---|---|---|---|
| P | Q | R | S | T |

| ᚢ | ᚦ | ᚹ | ᚦ | ᛃ |
|---|---|---|---|---|
| U | V | W | X | Y |

| | | ᛉ | | |
|---|---|---|---|---|
| | | Z | | |

# What's in a Name?

If you are unfamiliar with Anglo-Saxon names, here is a simple pronunciation guide. Just bear in mind that the stress should fall on the first syllable.

Aeshere – *Ash-hair-uh*

Beow – *Bay-oh*

Beowulf – *Bay-oh-wolf*

Breca – *Bray-car*

Edgetheow – *Edge-thay-ow*

Geat – *Gay-at*

Grendel – *Gren-del*

Handscio – *Hond-she-oh*

Healfdane – *Halph-day-nuh*

Heorot – *Hay-or-ot*

Hrothgar – *Hroath-gar*

Hrunting – *Hroont-ing*

Hygd – *Hoo-yud*

Hygelac – *Hoo-yuh-lark*

Naegling – *Nag-ling*

Scyld Scefing – *Shild Shay-fing*

Unferth – *Oon-ferth*

Wealhtheow – *Way-al-thee-ow*

Wiglaf – *Weeg-laugh*

Wulfgar – *Wolf-gar*

# Acknowledgements

There are a number of people who have joined me on my expedition to King Hrothgar's golden hall, and the subsequent voyage to Geatland, without whom this book would not be what it is.

First of all, a special mention must go to the illustrator, Russ Nicholson. To say it was a childhood dream come true, to have the talented artist who illustrated the first Fighting Fantasy gamebook, *The Warlock of Firetop Mountain*, collaborate on a project with me, would be something of an understatement. He has captured the historical setting of the story perfectly in the images he has produced for the book, and populated it with a host of enigmatic characters. And no one quite draws caves or smoke like Russ Nicholson!

Secondly, thank you to Emma Barnes at Snowbooks for her patience and support, and Anna Torborg for turning out such a fantastic-looking book.

I must also thank all those people who helped create the various Kickstarter rewards: Nicholas Zacharewicz, for the spoken passages of Old English in the Kickstarter promo video; Kevin Abbotts for the bookmarks and the hyperlinked eBook version of the adventure; Fil Baldowski of All Rolled Up for the dice trays and game rolls; and both Richard Scott of Otherworld Miniatures and sculptor Paul Muller for the fantastic models of Beowulf and Grendel.

I would also like to take this opportunity to thank two academics, who offered their advice and assistance during the writing of *Beowulf Beastslayer*. Firstly, Prof. Dr. Oliver M. Traxel, Professor of English Language and Linguistics at the University of Stavanger, for the Old English translations that appear throughout the adventure, and secondly Dr. Janina Ramirez, Course Director for the Undergraduate Certificate and Diploma in the History of Art at the University of Oxford, for her insights into the character of Beowulf and the cultural setting of the story.

But most importantly I offer a huge and heartfelt thank you to everyone who pledged their support to this venture from the outset and joined me on my journey back into the mythic past. Without them, this book would not exist. And so I raise my mead-horn to you and say, "Here's to you, the Kickstarter backers!"

# Kickstarter Backers

## Thralls

Jeffrey Dean • Antonio Campos Jr from McAllen Texas •
Bryan Howarth • Serenity Kaysdatter

## Huscarls

George Cayley

## Skalds

Adam Sparshott • Phil Ward • James Dickinson • Nash •
Christine Morgan • Meee • Ted Novy • Zombie Analectic •
Jeffrey Meyer • Simon Brake • Jonny Fontana •
Stuart Whitehouse • Cyril Keime • Silvano Oracolo •
Tommy Chu • James Smith • Ulrich Burmester •
Jay V. Schindler • Kat "Katastrophy9" Antinori •
Loki, Tilly & Murph • Robert Mills

## Karls

Mark Stoneham • Michael Hartley •
Zacharias Chun-pong LEUNG 梁振邦• Herman S. Skull •
Jason Baldwin • Rob Hodgson • Kirsty Skidmore •
Andrew Hartley • Mark Crew • Mark Lain •
Kamarul Azmi Kamaruzaman • Stuart Lloyd •
Vladimir 'Stigandr' Tierney • Zachary & Rachel Timmis •
Mark Taylor • Joe Tilbrook • Scott H. Moore • Frank Papalia •
Mark Lee Voss • Andy Barbieri • Stephen Redmond •
Craig Andrews • Paul Jones • Sue Lee •
WHO IS THE STEAM HIGHWAYMAN? • Pikey Berbil •
Dr Light • Ashton MacSaylor • Simon Hedley •
Alan Reid • Richard Harrison • Arthadan •
Amanda Jeffries • Nicodemus • Martin Gooch •
Andrew Wright • Annamarie Jennings •

David "the librarian" Stacey • Skorpio • Colin Deady •
Christopher Semler • Theo Clarke • Lucy Jefferies • N. Tanksley
• Mark Hirschman • Jason Hunter •
Javier Fernández-Sanguino • Luis Sanz •
Pang Peow Yeong & family • Devilman9050 •
Richard Bunting • Robertson Sondoh Jr • Chris Gardiner •
Mel Hall • Jon Ingold • Eric Priehs • Stephen Barr •
Jason Lenox @LenoxArtist • Brett Schofield •
Andrea "Ganesha games" Sfiligoi • Alistair Davidse •
Andrew Gilmartin • Matt Sheriff • Axel Riviere •
Henrik Gaardsted Spalk • Olivier Leclair • Murphorama •
Victor Cheng • Russell Owen • Craig Cousins •
Richie Aspie Stevens • Ori Ironarm • Natsutan •
Justin Whitman • Michael Stevens • Daniel Lee •
Ant O'Reilly • Joshua Abramsky • Caroline G. • Clay Skaggs
• John G. Gardiner • Jonathan L. Mendez • Chris Fong •
Sebastian D. • Scott Maxwell • Jennifer Brooks •
Paul Taylor • Chris Jefferson • Hana Honsová •
Xavier Van Den Nouwland • Konstanze Schaub Götzinger •
A. Donaghey • Ondřej Zástěra • Ken Boyter •
Štěpán Hofmeister • Gaetano Abbondanza • Tim Wild •
Godwin-Matthew Teoh Kok Wei • Gwyn • Ludvig •
Luke Sheridan • Trevor A. Ramirez • Sean Smith •
Vitas Varnas • Fiachra Delea • Paul Smith •
Arik (the Raider) Aslanyan • Heather Allen •
Lee A. Chrimes • Jarrad P. Wilkinson • Steve Lord • Ksprbgh •
Erik T. Johnson • Drakkar Darkholme • Paul Gaston •
J. Vonk • Gilles MANA • Jules Fattorini • Frederick Perillo•
Juha Johansson • Alex Mair • Timothy Haritun • Gary Nield •
Dane Barrett • Hans Peter Bak • Dave Morris •
Chuck McGrew •

# Jarls

Simon J. Painter • Colin Oaten • Michael Reilly •
Geoffrey Bertram • Ang NamLeng • Graham Hart •
Andrew Shannon • Paul, Noah, Jona & Elya Brueckner •
Chris Trapp • Ceiron Bounds • Phillip Bailey • Dave Bowen •
Matthew Lockman • Joe Grocott-James • Rob Crewe •
Marc Thorpe • Y. K. Lee • Scott William Sexton • Andy Bow •
Benjamin Wicka • Charles Revello • Brad Anderson •

Niki Lybæk • Anders Svensson • Vin de Silva •
Franck Teixido • Anthony Christopher Hackett •
Whiskey HotPot • Isabella De Leon • Stickfight •
Doug Thomson • Magnus Johansson • Jordan Burattini •
Robert H. Wilde • Luke Sanders • Aaron Clancy •
Antony McGarry-Thickitt • Matt Holvey • STEVEN PARRY •
Stéphane Bechard • Jess Vaughan • Edward Harvey Jr. •
Ken Nagasako • Robert M. Soderquist • Alexander Ballingall •
David Gillson • Ian McFarlin • Jontue Austin •
Robert T Carty, Jr. • James Aukett • Mario Villanueva •
Robin Horton • Francois Laisné

## Heralds

Jessica Taylor-Abbotts • James A. Hirons • Andrew Alvis •
Simon Day • Kola Krauze • Allan Matthews •
Michael Bailey • Rms • Lars Quante • René Batsford •
Mark "Daelhoof" Johnson • X. Zhao • Fabriec Gatille •
Eddie Boshell • Maggie Kulzer • Prof. Dr. Oliver M. Traxel •
Jason Vince (Dreamwalker Spirit) • Joe Kelly

## Heroes

Dominic Marcotte • Ian Greenfield • Fenric Cayne •
Jonathan Caines • John Dennis • Cato Vandrare • Judykins •
Per Stalby • Adrian Jankowiak • David J. Williams •
Carl Radley • Naab • Jeremy R. Haupt • Anonymous •
Ian "Geronimo" Brumby • Thomas Dan Nielsen •
Stefano Mazza • Sapper Joe • Jason Gross

## Kings

林立人 Lin Liren • Simon Scott • Luca Meregalli •
Gonçalo Rodrigues • David Poppel • Ron Bishop •
ジャックタン

# About the Author

Jonathan Green is a writer of speculative fiction, with more than seventy books to his name. Well known for his contributions to the Fighting Fantasy range of adventure gamebooks, he has also written fiction for such diverse properties as *Doctor Who, Star Wars: The Clone Wars, Warhammer, Warhammer 40,000, Sonic the Hedgehog, Teenage Mutant Ninja Turtles, Moshi Monsters, LEGO, Judge Dredd, Robin of Sherwood,* and *Frostgrave.*

He is the creator of the *Pax Britannia* series for Abaddon Books and has written eight novels and numerous short stories set within this steampunk universe, featuring the debonair dandy adventurer Ulysses Quicksilver. He is also the author of an increasing number of non-fiction titles, including the award-winning *YOU ARE THE HERO – A History of Fighting Fantasy Gamebooks* series.

He occasionally edits and compiles short story anthologies, such as the critically-acclaimed *GAME OVER, SHARKPUNK,* and *Shakespeare Vs Cthulhu,* all of which are published by Snowbooks.

To find out more about ACE Gamebooks and his other projects, visit www.JonathanGreenAuthor.com and follow him on Twitter @jonathangreen.

# BEOWULF BEASTSLAYER
## ADVENTURE SHEET

AGILITY

MEALS

COMBAT

CREW

ENDURANCE

HERO POINTS

EQUIPMENT

KENNINGS

# BEOWULF
## ENCOUNTERS BOXES

COMBAT=
ENDURANCE=

COMBAT=
ENDURANCE=

COMBAT=
ENDURANCE=

COMBAT=
ENDURANCE=

COMBAT=
ENDURANCE=

COMBAT=
ENDURANCE=

COMBAT=
ENDURANCE=

COMBAT=
ENDURANCE=

COMBAT=
ENDURANCE=

COMBAT=
ENDURANCE=

# BEOWULF
## ENCOUNTERS BOXES

COMBAT=
ENDURANCE=

COMBAT=
ENDURANCE=

COMBAT=
ENDURANCE=

COMBAT=
ENDURANCE=

COMBAT=
ENDURANCE=

COMBAT=
ENDURANCE=

COMBAT=
ENDURANCE=

COMBAT=
ENDURANCE=

COMBAT=
ENDURANCE=

COMBAT=
ENDURANCE=

# BEOWULF BEASTSLAYER
## ADVENTURE SHEET

AGILITY

MEALS

COMBAT

CREW

ENDURANCE

HERO POINTS

EQUIPMENT

KENNINGS

# BEOWULF
## ENCOUNTERS BOXES

COMBAT=
ENDURANCE=

COMBAT=
ENDURANCE=

COMBAT=
ENDURANCE=

COMBAT=
ENDURANCE=

COMBAT=
ENDURANCE=

COMBAT=
ENDURANCE=

COMBAT=
ENDURANCE=

COMBAT=
ENDURANCE=

COMBAT=
ENDURANCE=

COMBAT=
ENDURANCE=

# BEOWULF
## ENCOUNTERS BOXES

COMBAT=
ENDURANCE=

COMBAT=
ENDURANCE=

COMBAT=
ENDURANCE=

COMBAT=
ENDURANCE=

COMBAT=
ENDURANCE=

COMBAT=
ENDURANCE=

COMBAT=
ENDURANCE=

COMBAT=
ENDURANCE=

COMBAT=
ENDURANCE=

COMBAT=
ENDURANCE=

# BEOWULF BEASTSLAYER
## ADVENTURE SHEET

AGILITY

MEALS

COMBAT

CREW

ENDURANCE

HERO POINTS

EQUIPMENT

KENNINGS

# BEOWULF
## ENCOUNTERS BOXES

COMBAT=
ENDURANCE=

COMBAT=
ENDURANCE=

COMBAT=
ENDURANCE=

COMBAT=
ENDURANCE=

COMBAT=
ENDURANCE=

COMBAT=
ENDURANCE=

COMBAT=
ENDURANCE=

COMBAT=
ENDURANCE=

COMBAT=
ENDURANCE=

COMBAT=
ENDURANCE=

# BEOWULF
## ENCOUNTERS BOXES

COMBAT=
ENDURANCE=

COMBAT=
ENDURANCE=

COMBAT=
ENDURANCE=

COMBAT=
ENDURANCE=

COMBAT=
ENDURANCE=

COMBAT=
ENDURANCE=

COMBAT=
ENDURANCE=

COMBAT=
ENDURANCE=

COMBAT=
ENDURANCE=

COMBAT=
ENDURANCE=

# BEOWULF BEASTSLAYER
## ADVENTURE SHEET

AGILITY

MEALS

COMBAT

CREW

ENDURANCE

HERO POINTS

EQUIPMENT

KENNINGS

# BEOWULF
## ENCOUNTERS BOXES

COMBAT=
ENDURANCE=

COMBAT=
ENDURANCE=

COMBAT=
ENDURANCE=

COMBAT=
ENDURANCE=

COMBAT=
ENDURANCE=

COMBAT=
ENDURANCE=

COMBAT=
ENDURANCE=

COMBAT=
ENDURANCE=

COMBAT=
ENDURANCE=

COMBAT=
ENDURANCE=

# BEOWULF
## ENCOUNTERS BOXES

COMBAT=
ENDURANCE=

COMBAT=
ENDURANCE=

COMBAT=
ENDURANCE=

COMBAT=
ENDURANCE=

COMBAT=
ENDURANCE=

COMBAT=
ENDURANCE=

COMBAT=
ENDURANCE=

COMBAT=
ENDURANCE=

COMBAT=
ENDURANCE=

COMBAT=
ENDURANCE=

# BEOWULF BEASTSLAYER
## ADVENTURE SHEET

AGILITY

MEALS

COMBAT

CREW

ENDURANCE

HERO POINTS

EQUIPMENT

KENNINGS

# BEOWULF
## ENCOUNTERS BOXES

COMBAT=
ENDURANCE=

COMBAT=
ENDURANCE=

COMBAT=
ENDURANCE=

COMBAT=
ENDURANCE=

COMBAT=
ENDURANCE=

COMBAT=
ENDURANCE=

COMBAT=
ENDURANCE=

COMBAT=
ENDURANCE=

COMBAT=
ENDURANCE=

COMBAT=
ENDURANCE=

# BEOWULF
## ENCOUNTERS BOXES

COMBAT=
ENDURANCE=

COMBAT=
ENDURANCE=

COMBAT=
ENDURANCE=

COMBAT=
ENDURANCE=

COMBAT=
ENDURANCE=

COMBAT=
ENDURANCE=

COMBAT=
ENDURANCE=

COMBAT=
ENDURANCE=

COMBAT=
ENDURANCE=

COMBAT=
ENDURANCE=

# ALSO FROM
# JONATHAN GREEN

# THE WICKED WIZARD OF OZ

## A CHOOSE YOUR PATH ADVENTURE GAMEBOOK

## JONATHAN GREEN

### ILLUSTRATED BY KEV CROSSLEY